D0836737

FROM THE
NANCY DREW FILES

THE CASE: Nancy investigates the suspicious death of Davis Field's top-rated flight trainee, Jill Parker.

CONTACT: Admiral Martin Lewis, base commander, asks Nancy to go undercover as a jet fighter trainee.

SUSPECTS: Crash Beauford—He says women don't deserve to be fighter pilots . . . especially one like Jill, who was rated a better flyer than he.

Steven Eriksen—He represents Aerotech, whose multimillion-dollar contract with the navy was threatened by Jill's computer research.

Mary Chambers—A trainee who had a lot in common with the victim . . . including an ex-boyfriend who became Jill's husband.

COMPLICATIONS: Looking for trouble? Look no further than Crash Beauford. So what is it that Nancy finds so appealing about him?

Books in The Nancy Drew Files™ Series

#1	SECRETS CAN KILL	#68	CROSSCURRENTS
#2	DEADLY INTENT	#70	CUTTING EDGE
#3	MURDER ON ICE	#71	HOT TRACKS
#4	SMILE AND SAY MURDER	#72	SWISS SECRETS
#5	HIT AND RUN HOLIDAY	#73	RENDEZVOUS IN ROME
#6	WHITE WATER TERROR	#74	GREEK ODYSSEY
#7	DEADLY DOUBLES	#75	A TALENT FOR MURDER
#8	TWO POINTS TO MURDER	#76	THE PERFECT PLOT
#9	FALSE MOVES	#77	DANGER ON PARADE
#10	BURIED SECRETS	#78	UPDATE ON CRIME
#11	HEART OF DANGER	#79	NO LAUGHING MATTER
#16	NEVER SAY DIE	#80	POWER OF SUGGESTION
#17	STAY TUNED FOR DANGER	#81	MAKING WAVES
#19	SISTERS IN CRIME	#82	DANGEROUS RELATIONS
#31	TROUBLE IN TAHITI	#83	DIAMOND DECEIT
#35	BAD MEDICINE	#84	CHOOSING SIDES
#36	OVER THE EDGE	#85	SEA OF SUSPICION
#37	LAST DANCE	#86	LET'S TALK TERROR
#41	SOMETHING TO HIDE	#87	MOVING TARGET
#43	FALSE IMPRESSIONS	#88	FALSE PRETENSES
#45	OUT OF BOUNDS	#89	DESIGNS IN CRIME
#46	WIN, PLACE OR DIE	#90	STAGE FRIGHT
#49	PORTRAIT IN CRIME	#91	IF LOOKS COULD KILL
#50	DEEP SECRETS	#92	MY DEADLY VALENTINE
#51	A MODEL CRIME	#93	HOTLINE TO DANGER
#53	TRAIL OF LIES	#94	ILLUSIONS OF EVIL
#54	COLD AS ICE	#95	AN INSTINCT FOR TROUBLE
#55	DON'T LOOK TWICE	#96	THE RUNAWAY BRIDE
#56	MAKE NO MISTAKE	#97	SQUEEZE PLAY
#57	INTO THIN AIR	#98	ISLAND OF SECRETS
#58	HOT PURSUIT	#99	THE CHEATING HEART
#59	HIGH RISK	#100	DANCE TILL YOU DIE
#60	POISON PEN	#101	THE PICTURE OF GUILT
#61	SWEET REVENGE	#102	COUNTERFEIT CHRISTMAS
#62	EASY MARKS	#103	HEART OF ICE
#63	MIXED SIGNALS	#104	KISS AND TELL
#64	THE WRONG TRACK	#105	STOLEN AFFECTIONS
#65	FINAL NOTES	#106	FLYING TOO HIGH
#66	TALL, DARK AND DEADLY		

Available from ARCHWAY Paperbacks

COLOMA PUBLIC LIBRARY

30151000394069

JUN 28 '95

JUL 13 '95   AUG

AP 11 '95
  AUG 12 '95
  SEP 13 '95

NOV 2 '95

NOV 23 '95

MAR 8 '96

MAR 26 '96

JUN 21 '96

AUG 25 '97

The
NANCY DREW

FLYING

CAROL

DATE DUE

MY 18 '06

NO 08 '18
NO 29 '18

DE 18 '18

Demco, Inc. 38-294

AP 15

AN ARCH
Published
New York   London

COLOMA PUBLIC LIBRARY

The sale of this book without its cover is unauthorized. If you purchased this book without a cover, you should be aware that it was reported to the publisher as "unsold and destroyed." Neither the author nor the publisher has received payment for the sale of this "stripped book."

This book is a work of fiction. Names, characters, places and incidents are products of the author's imagination or are used fictitiously. Any resemblance to actual events or locales or persons, living or dead, is entirely coincidental.

AN ARCHWAY PAPERBACK *Original*

An Archway Paperback published by
POCKET BOOKS, a division of Simon & Schuster Inc.
1230 Avenue of the Americas, New York, NY 10020

Copyright © 1995 by Simon & Schuster Inc.
Produced by Mega-Books, Inc.

All rights reserved, including the right to reproduce
this book or portions thereof in any form whatsoever.
For information address Pocket Books, 1230 Avenue
of the Americas, New York, NY 10020

ISBN: 0-671-88197-3

First Archway Paperback printing April 1995

10 9 8 7 6 5 4 3 2 1

NANCY DREW, AN ARCHWAY PAPERBACK and colophon
are registered trademarks of Simon & Schuster Inc.

THE NANCY DREW FILES is a trademark of
Simon & Schuster Inc.

Cover art by Cliff Miller

Printed in the U.S.A.

IL 6+

FLYING TOO HIGH

Chapter

One

"SUN, SURF, AND SAND . . ." George Fayne turned briefly from behind the wheel of the white convertible rental car to grin at Nancy Drew. "This is the kind of case I like!"

"Hmm?" Nancy looked up from the dog-eared manual in her lap, taking in the brilliant white sand that edged the highway. To their right sunlight glinted off the Gulf of Mexico, and a warm breeze ruffled Nancy's reddish blond hair, which was pulled back in a loose French braid. "This part of the Florida coast *is* beautiful. I've been too busy preparing for this case to notice."

"That's understandable," George said, pushing back her short dark curls with her sunglasses, which were propped on top of her head. "Going undercover in the U.S. Navy can't be easy for someone with no military training."

1

"It's definitely a challenge. I'm glad Admiral Lewis sent someone to River Heights to give me a crash course in 'the navy way,'" Nancy said, "but there's still so much to know. I hope I can pull it off."

"Well, you certainly look the part," George said, eyeing Nancy's dark blue ensign's uniform.

A week earlier Nancy's father had been contacted by Admiral Martin Lewis, who'd been a neighbor of the Drews in River Heights. The admiral was now the commander at Davis Field Naval Air Station, on the Florida panhandle.

"Admiral Lewis didn't tell Dad exactly what we'll be investigating—just that there's been trouble in the fighter pilot training program and that he wants someone from outside to look into it," Nancy explained. "Since I know how to fly—"

"You get the job," George finished. "So what kind of experience do the other trainees have?"

Nancy took a deep breath to recite all the credentials the trainees had to have. "To start with, a trainee has to have graduated from college, the Naval Academy, or ROTC. From there, the best students go on to AOCS—Aviation Officer Candidate School. That's where I was supposed to have gone through basic training and API—"

"Wait a sec. You lost me," George interrupted. "What's API?"

"Aviation Pilot Indoctrination," Nancy answered. "Learning the basics, plus learning about

2

military science and the navy's rules and regulations."

George let out a low whistle. "No wonder you've been studying so much."

"There's more, too. After AOCS, trainees go to Davis Field for four weeks of ground school and training in CPTs," Nancy went on.

"More initials?" George asked, groaning.

"CPTs are Cockpit Trainers," Nancy explained, laughing. "They're stationary cockpits that trainees use to learn basic flying procedures, like taking off and landing. At this point, there still hasn't been any actual flying. That doesn't come until the part of the training I'm entering."

Nancy waved the manual in her lap. "This is full of flying specifications I have to know for my in-the-air training. How to do spins, dead-air landings, touching down on an aircraft carrier . . ."

"I suppose there's an acronym for *that* part of the training, too?" George asked dryly.

"This is called the NATOPS manual," Nancy answered, grinning. "That stands for Navy Aviation Training Operation Standards. The planes I'll be using don't have fighting capabilities. It takes several months before trainees move on to real fighter planes."

"Sounds pretty impressive, but I think you forgot to tell me about the most important part of the training program," George said. "The CGA."

"CGA?" The initials didn't mean a thing.

Nancy worried that she had overlooked important background material, until she saw the half grin on George's face.

"Cute Guy Alert," George supplied, and laughed out loud. "From what I understand, the ratio of guys to girls in the military is definitely in the girls' favor."

Nancy smiled. "I've already got a boyfriend, remember?" she said. "Anyway, even if I wasn't dating Ned, I'd be too busy investigating to pay attention to guys."

She nodded to the left at a chain-link fence that ran close to the road. Signs along the fence read Restricted Area—U.S. Navy. Set far back from the road were dozens of metal and concrete buildings. A plane was just arcing into the sky behind them. "This must be the place," Nancy said.

A minute later George turned into the entrance to Davis Field Naval Air Station and stopped at the security gate. After checking their names on a list, the guard waved them through and gave them directions to Admiral Lewis's office. They wound past a few concrete buildings before arriving at a complex of squat brick buildings surrounded by lawns and flowering shrubs.

After getting out of the car, Nancy put on her navy blue cap, squared her shoulders, and took a deep breath. "The one thing Admiral Lewis *did* tell me is that we're undercover from the second we're on the base. No one except he and his secretary knows our real reason for being here.

So from now on, I'm Ensign Drew, and you're a friend of mine who works in the admiral's office."

"Got it." George gave Nancy a half salute, then said, "Lead on, Ensign."

A secretary with wavy brown hair and a pleasant smile sat at a desk outside of Admiral Lewis's office. When Nancy and George told her who they were, she pressed an intercom button. Seconds later Admiral Lewis appeared in the doorway of his office.

Nancy snapped to attention and gave a crisp salute. "Sir! Ensign Nancy Drew reporting for duty, sir."

"And this young woman is George Fayne," the secretary added, nodding toward George.

"Thank you, Fran." Nancy noticed the sparkle in the admiral's brown eyes as he gave her a return salute, then shook George's hand. "Ensign. Miss Fayne. Please come in."

It had been several years since Nancy had last seen Admiral Lewis. His short black hair was grayer than she remembered, but he still had the same cocoa-colored skin, strong angular face, and warm brown eyes. Even though he was in his sixties, he had a powerful, muscular build. In his formal, dark blue navy uniform he was an imposing figure of authority. As soon as the three of them were inside his office, the admiral closed the door and gestured for Nancy and George to sit in two chairs in front of his desk. Then he walked around and sat behind the desk and folded his hands on the neat, polished wood surface. "I want to thank you for coming on such short notice."

"We're glad to help out," George told him.

The admiral gave them each a smile, then said, "Nancy, based on the fine salute I just saw, you've gotten a feel for the navy's way of doing things. Your training with Gunnery Sergeant McDaniel went well?"

Nancy knew what he was really asking: Would she be able to convince the other trainees in the fighter pilot program that she had had the same rigorous training they'd had? "I've been walking, talking, eating, sleeping, and dreaming navy for the last week," she told the admiral. "And I memorized the training background you and Sergeant McDaniel made up for me. I'm as ready as I can be."

"Good," he said approvingly. "Now . . ." He pushed a manila file across his desk toward her and George. "This is the full background information on the case, but in a nutshell, Jill Banks Parker, one of our most talented trainees, was killed in a plane crash last week. The official report cited engine failure as the cause of the crash."

"But you're not so sure it was an accident?" George guessed.

"I'm afraid that report might be a bunch a hogwash," Admiral Lewis answered bluntly. Fixing Nancy and George with his direct gaze, he explained, "As you know, women were not allowed to become fighter pilots until recently. We had a tough time adjusting at first, but now just about everyone is proud that women have joined the fighter pilot training program. Still, I can't rule out the possibility that Jill may have been killed by one of the few people who are still against women fighter pilots."

"Or that if the person who wrote the report didn't like having women in the fighter pilot program, he might have . . . overlooked evidence of sabotage?" George added.

The admiral nodded. "The report was written by Lieutenant Commander Styles. He was at one of our bases on Guam when Jill's plane crashed, so he couldn't have been directly involved in any foul play. I've always considered him a good man—no reason to believe he'd overlook damaging evidence, but . . . well, I owe it to the navy *and* to Jill's husband to make sure the report is accurate."

This obviously wasn't easy for him, Nancy thought. "Are there any special facts that led you to think Jill's death might *not* have been accidental?" she asked.

"Before Jill died, she showed her On Wing some anonymous threats she'd received," Admiral Lewis said.

George's expression reflected her confusion. "Her On Wing? What's that?"

"An On Wing is a *who*, actually," Nancy explained. "The officer Jill was doing her one-on-one flight training with." Turning to the admiral, she asked, "Aren't On Wings supposed to go up with trainees whenever they fly? Was Jill's On Wing in the crash, too?"

Admiral Lewis nodded soberly. "He was luckier than Jill. He sustained serious head wounds, but he survived. Unfortunately, he has no memory whatsoever of the flight."

"So he can't tell us anything that could lead us to whoever might have sabotaged the plane," Nancy said, thinking out loud.

"I'm not convinced that anyone *did* sabotage the plane," the admiral put in quickly. "That's why I brought you in—so I can get an impartial report."

Nancy knew there were so many things she needed to check before she could write that report. "I'd like to start by seeing the plane Jill was flying—and the notes she received."

"I'll set up clearance for you to visit the plane. The notes are in the file, along with Lieutenant Commander Styles's report," Admiral Lewis said. "Jill lived in a house in town with the three other women in her training class, Ensigns Chambers, Watts, and Vega. I've arranged for you to take over Jill's room."

"Great," Nancy told him. "Am I going to join her training class?"

The admiral shook his head. "Jill's class has been at Davis Field for over a month. Most of the trainees are at a fairly advanced stage in their initial training—I'm afraid there's no way for you to join that class without arousing suspicion.

I've arranged for you to enter a new class starting this week. You'll have access to all the same planes and equipment. Apart from flight times and sessions on the computer simulators, you will have plenty of unscheduled time. Lots of opportunities to investigate."

"Sounds good," Nancy said.

"George, you'll be working in this office," Admiral Lewis went on. "As my assistant, you'll have access to any files or records Nancy might need. Mrs. Lewis has fixed up our guest room for you, and she's offered to lend you her car so you can get around."

"Thanks," George said, grinning at the admiral. "You've really thought of everything."

"I hope so. One thing you'll learn about us navy types—we like to be prepared." Admiral Lewis glanced at his watch before getting to his feet. "Nancy, you're scheduled to start your first familiarization class, FAM-O, at the south airfield at thirteen hundred hours."

The navy used a twenty-four-hour clock, Nancy knew. Thirteen hundred hours was one o'clock in the afternoon, just ten minutes away.

"Your On Wing is Lieutenant Rhonda Kisch." Raising an eyebrow, the admiral added, "She's no marshmallow, Nancy. If I were you, I'd be on time."

"Sir! Ensign Nancy Drew reporting for duty, sir!"

Nancy wondered how many times she was

going to have to repeat that phrase while at Davis Field. She'd run across the entire base in order to get to the south airfield on time. She was hot and sweaty, and a few wisps of her hair had come undone from her French braid. As she stood at attention just outside the hangar, she could feel her On Wing's critical gaze taking in her every imperfection.

It wasn't until Lieutenant Kisch saluted and told Nancy she could be "at ease," that Nancy was able to really look at her. Rhonda Kisch was a few inches shorter than Nancy's five feet seven inches. She had a curvy build that was emphasized by her uniform. She wore no makeup, and her blond hair was cut blunt in a short, no-nonsense style. Nancy guessed that she was in her early thirties, but it was hard to tell. The stern expression in the lieutenant's gray eyes told Nancy she was all business.

"The purpose of today's session is to get to know each other and to see what you know about the plane you'll be flying," Lieutenant Kisch began. Her crisp, curt voice held the slightest hint of a Southern accent. "We won't be going up in the air until FAM-One, our next familiarization session."

While she spoke, she led Nancy into the hangar, a huge open building housing over a dozen planes. There were a few other navy personnel inside, but Lieutenant Kisch didn't pay any attention to them. She stepped over to the closest plane and patted the outside of the cockpit. "Tell me what kind of plane we have here, Ensign."

"It's a T-thirty-four C, a single-engine, turbo-prop plane that's commonly called the Mentor," Nancy began. As she rattled off the information she'd memorized, she noticed a tall woman getting into the front seat of one of the other planes. Black hair peeked from beneath her safety helmet, and she wore the olive zip-up coverall that was required flight attire for all trainees. A man in his thirties who was probably the girl's On Wing climbed into the rear position. The engine started with a deafening roar, and Nancy had to stop talking while the plane taxied out of the hangar and onto the runway. Moments later the noise deepened to supersonic intensity as the plane sped down the runway and angled up into the cloudless sky.

"Ensign Drew!"

Nancy snapped back to focus on her On Wing, then groaned inwardly when she saw the scowl on Lieutenant Kisch's face. "You're not here to stand around. Keep your mind on what you're doing," the lieutenant barked.

"Yes, sir!"

"I'm going to clue you in on something, Ensign," Lieutenant Kisch went on. "The navy is a man's world. In order to excel, women have to be tougher, smarter, and faster than our male counterparts. Think you're up to the challenge?"

Nancy saluted and said, "Yes, sir!" again. But

judging by the dubious glimmer in Lieutenant Kisch's eyes, the On Wing didn't believe her.

"Then start acting like it."

Nancy bristled but didn't say anything. She wouldn't have thought that watching another plane take off was being lazy. With a sigh, Nancy climbed into the open cockpit behind the lieutenant.

For the next hour, the On Wing grilled her on the operation of the T-34C, the layout of the airfield, and the flight patterns of the area. Nancy got most of the information right, but there was so much to know that she had to stop to think a few times.

"I don't have all day, Ensign," the lieutenant said after Nancy hesitated on one answer. She snapped her fingers several times in rapid succession. "Let's get on the ball. Tell me again—what's the layout of the south airfield?"

They were standing outside the hangar now, and most of the base's buildings were behind them. Nancy gazed south at the flat expanse of runway, palms, and sandy soil, trying to remember the geography of the south field. "Okay, Airstrip Number One angles northwest to southeast. . . ."

As she spoke, Nancy caught sight of the plane she'd seen take off earlier. It flew toward the base from offshore, then got into position to land. Nancy forced herself to keep her mind on her explanation. "Just behind those trees is the Gulf of Mexico. . . ."

Her eyes flitted back to the plane in the sky, and she broke off with a gasp. "Something's wrong!"

The plane was banking around to come parallel with the landing strip, but instead of turning smoothly, the plane began to waver unsteadily.

"Ensign," Lieutenant Kisch said sternly, "I thought I told you—" Then she frowned up at the plane. "Something *is* wrong," she said.

The plane's nose had dipped dangerously. A moment later the Mentor began spinning in the air, heading right for the ground.

"The plane's out of control!" Nancy yelled. "It's going to crash!"

Chapter

Two

Nancy watched helplessly as the plane plummeted toward the landing strip. Shouts rose up from the hangar. "What's the matter!" "Oh, no!" "That Mentor's going to crash!"

Just when Nancy thought the plane would surely hit, the pilot managed to get it under control. With a shaky twist, the plane picked up altitude and shot over the base, then turned around to try the landing again. Nancy's eyes were glued to the Mentor. She hardly dared breathe as it banked and angled lower and lower. This time, the pilot remained in control and the plane touched down perfectly.

Nancy waited for her On Wing to yell at her for becoming distracted, but Lieutenant Kisch's attention remained on the plane that had just landed. She watched silently as the Mentor taxied to the hangar. When the trainee and her On Wing climbed down from the cockpit, Lieutenant Kisch hurried over to them. "What happened up there, Lou?" the lieutenant asked the other On Wing.

The On Wing, a tall man with dark brown skin and high cheekbones, was frowning as he pulled off his safety helmet. "What's your guess, Ensign Chambers?" he asked the dark-haired trainee.

Nancy recognized the woman's name. Ensign Chambers would be one of her housemates. The young woman had short black hair, big brown eyes, and a high forehead. She appeared to be very shaken. "Sir, I don't *know* what happened!" she wailed. "All of a sudden my computer controls weren't working and we were spinning out of control. I swear I didn't do anything wrong!"

"It's all right, Ensign," the On Wing said. "The important thing is that we're all right." Turning to Lieutenant Kisch, he explained, "My controls were okay, so I was able to bring us down safely."

Nancy knew that the Mentor had two sets of flying controls, and that both sets had computerized components. While the two On Wings began a thorough inspection of the plane, Nancy stepped over to the other trainee. "Hi, I'm Nancy Drew. I'm starting my training this week."

"I'm Mary Chambers," the other girl said with a shaky smile. She blinked, looking at Nancy more closely. "Drew? Aren't you the girl who's going to take over Jill's room—" She broke off uncertainly. "You heard what happened?"

Nancy nodded. "I was really sorry to hear about the accident," she said truthfully. "Doesn't it seem weird that first Jill's plane crashes, and then yours almost does?"

"Tell me about it," Mary said, her eyes opening wide. "I'm starting to get the creeps!"

Was Mary trying to say that she suspected foul play? Nancy decided to probe a little. "So you don't think it's just coincidence?" she asked Mary.

Mary's brown eyes narrowed, and her jaw became set in a hard line. "Jill's crash was an accident. I'm sure this was, too," she said firmly, then turned and went to a wall of lockers.

Whoa! Nancy thought, following Mary with her eyes. Mary had completely clammed up when Nancy hinted at the possibility of foul play. Nancy knew she was hiding something, but what?

"It looks as if Mary was right. There was some sort of breakdown of the computer components," Mary's On Wing said, breaking into Nancy's thoughts.

"Why do you think they suddenly stopped working?" Nancy asked.

"The experts will have to examine the components before we know the answer to that question," Nancy's On Wing answered.

She was interrupted by the sound of deep laughter behind her. Turning around, Nancy saw three young men in flight gear sauntering toward Mary Chambers. "Nice job, Chambers," one of the men said to Mary. He was tall, with short dark hair. Mirrored sunglasses hid his eyes, but there was no missing the sarcasm in his voice. He turned to the other two guys and added, "The navy's in big trouble now that women drivers are up in the air—"

Mary's cheeks turned red. Before she could reply, Lieutenant Kisch snapped, "Ensign Beauford! *What* did I just hear you say?"

The young man snapped to attention. "It was nothing, sir," he said.

Lieutenant Kisch strode over to the three guys, never taking her eyes off their faces. "Good. Because if I heard you treat any of the women on this base with anything less than absolute respect, I would report it directly to Admiral Lewis."

"Yes, sir." The dark-haired young man waited at attention until he was excused. Then he and the other two guys left the hangar. Lieutenant Kisch watched them briefly, then turned to Nancy.

"We're not through with our session yet, Ensign. You were describing the layout of the south field."

"Yes, sir," Nancy answered, having a hard time concentrating on her explanation. The three male trainees she'd just seen had made it very clear that it *was* tough for women in the fighter pilot training program. Now Lieutenant Kisch was making it even tougher with her relentless questions.

Between solving the case *and* keeping up with my training, Nancy thought, I'm going to have my hands full.

It was four o'clock by the time Nancy's familiarization session ended and she made it back to Admiral Lewis's office to pick up her car and the directions to her house. As she made her way up the stairs to the admiral's office, Nancy thought about Mary Chambers's near accident. Her gut instincts told her it *wasn't* an accident. But if Mary were a victim, why did she act so unwilling to admit that someone might have sabotaged her plane or Jill's?

"Oh! Excuse me." Nancy had been so lost in thought that she didn't notice the man who was coming down the metal stairs. He wore glasses and had white hair that was slicked back over the tanned, balding crown of his head. A plastic civilian pass was clipped to the lapel of his gray suit. He nodded distractedly at Nancy as she stepped around him and continued up the stairs.

When Nancy got to Admiral Lewis's outer office, George was standing in front of the filing cabinet next to the secretary's desk. Fran wasn't there, but a dark-haired man was leaning against the desk talking to George while she filed some papers. Neither of them noticed Nancy until she was right next to them.

"Hi, Nancy!" George said brightly, turning toward her. "How did your training session go?"

"It was interesting," Nancy answered vaguely,

not wanting to talk about the case in front of a stranger.

"Richard, this is Ensign Nancy Drew, the friend I was telling you about." An excited flush rose on George's cheeks. "Nan, meet Richard Mirsky."

Nancy gave Richard a closer look as she shook his hand. She guessed that he was only a few years older than she and George. He was tall, about five feet eleven inches, with dark curly hair, pale blue eyes, and a closely cropped beard. He had an athletic build and wore a sports jacket and button-down shirt over tan slacks. Nancy didn't miss the appreciative glint in his eyes when he stared at George.

"Nice to meet you," Nancy told him. "What are you doing here at Davis Field?"

Richard tapped the visitors' pass clipped to his jacket. "Just some research," he said good-naturedly.

"Richard's writing an article on the computer simulation programs they use in fighter pilot training," George went on.

George didn't get bubbly and flirtatious around guys, the way her cousin Bess Marvin did, but every once in a while she met a guy who made her act a little—different. Right then George was glowing in a way Nancy hadn't seen in a while.

George finished filing her papers, and then she, Nancy, and Richard left together. When they got to the parking lot, Richard stopped next to a blue hatchback. "Here's my trusty horse," he said. "It was nice meeting you, Nancy. George, I'll pick you up at seven, okay?"

"See you then." George's tone was casual, but Nancy noticed the slight color that rose to her cheeks. As they walked away, Nancy raised an eyebrow at her friend. "Sounds like a date."

George shrugged. "We're just having dinner," she said. "You don't mind, do you? I mean, I figured you'd be busy meeting the other fighter pilot trainees, but if you want me to help you do some investigating . . ."

"I don't mind," Nancy assured her. She added, "Anyway, I don't blame you for wanting to get to know Richard better. He's cute. And he's definitely interested in you."

The color in George's cheeks deepened. "You think so?" she asked. Then she shook herself. "Oh! I almost forgot, we have clearance to examine Jill's plane. It's in a hangar at the east field—Number Four. All we have to do is show our passes to the guard."

"Great. After that I'd better go meet my housemates," Nancy said as she and George got in the rented convertible. After consulting her map of the base, Nancy started the car and headed toward the east airfield. While she drove, she filled George in on what had happened. "Admiral Lewis should have the plane checked out by someone he trusts," she finished.

"I'll tell him about it," George said worriedly.

"This case could be more dangerous than we imagined, Nan. Be careful."

"I always am," Nancy assured her. They had reached the east airfield, and Nancy parked near a row of hangars. Nancy grabbed her file and she and George started down the row of hangars. About halfway down was Hangar Number Four, closed with a guard in front. When Nancy and George showed the guard their passes, he unlocked a small metal door set into the wall near the huge rolling metal gate.

Once the guard had closed the door behind them, Nancy paused to take in the space. Two rows of planes stood at the far end of the hangar. Closer to them was the wreckage of a T-34C.

"Wow," George whispered, her eyes wide.

The nose of the plane was completely smashed and charred. One wing had snapped off completely, while the other was severely damaged. Nancy gazed in through the cracked and twisted cockpit door. The control panel for the front position, the one where the trainee sat, was nothing more than a charred mass of knobs and buttons. The rear position was in better condition. It was burned only slightly, and the controls on its panel were recognizable.

"Admiral Lewis was right when he said that Jill's On Wing was lucky," George said, shaking her head. "It's hard to believe *anyone* could live through this."

"Or that anyone would have intentionally

caused the crash," Nancy added soberly. She opened her file, and her gaze fell on two notes typed on plain notepaper. The words *FLYING CAN BE DANGEROUS TO YOUR HEALTH* were typed on the first, while the second read, *NOSY GIRLS FINISH LAST*.

"Those threats aren't very specific," George said, peeking over Nancy's shoulder.

"No," Nancy agreed. "And this paper is very common. Maybe Lieutenant Commander Styles's report will give us more to go on."

After setting the notes aside, she began reading the typed report. The report stated that severe engine damage indicated engine malfunction, but that the destruction was so widespread that it was impossible to know with certainty the precise cause of the malfunction. Since there was no obvious evidence of tampering, he concluded that the crash was accidental.

When she was finished reading the report, Nancy handed the folder to George, then stepped closer to the plane. "I'm going to start my own search," she said. "If I see anything that contradicts this report, there's a good chance that Lieutenant Commander Styles is covering up something."

While George took a turn reading the report, Nancy climbed up to the cockpit and bent over the charred controls. Taking a pen from the pocket of her uniform, she poked gingerly at them. "Pressure gauge—throttle—altitude gyro —radio magnetic indicator—"

Everything was so mangled it was impossible to tell what many of the charred metal bits were. With a sigh, she gave up. Stepping down from the cockpit, she opened the metal panel at the side of the plane that revealed the engine and fuel system—and let out a low whistle.

Whoa! she thought to herself, staring at the shattered hunks of metal. This engine didn't just malfunction—it blew up! She reached into a pocket and pulled out her penlight, then shined it at the grease-covered pieces of burned metal. The shattered bits had blown away from the engine and glued themselves against the fuel lines and inside the plane's outer shell.

Just as she was about to give up trying to identify the metal bits, something wedged behind the shattered engine caught her attention. She picked at the bit of metal, then pulled out the remains of a metal watch. "George! Look at this!" Nancy turned and held out the watch.

Seconds later George climbed behind her on the ladder. "A watch? What's *that* doing in the engine?"

"I don't know, but I'd be willing to bet it was a man who left it. It looks like it had a pretty wide strap, and it's a style that's too clunky for a woman's watch," Nancy said, thinking out loud. "What I don't get is *why* anyone would leave it there."

"And why didn't Lieutenant Commander Styles find it when he examined the wreck?" George added. "Maybe—"

Abruptly Nancy held up a hand to silence George. "Shh! I think I heard something!" she whispered, jerking her head around to the rear of the hangar.

They both stood completely still, listening. A moment later she heard it again—the scuffling of shoes along the hangar's concrete floor.

"Nancy," George gasped, grabbing Nancy's arm. "Someone's listening to us!"

Chapter

Three

"WHO'S THERE?" Nancy demanded, her voice echoing in the cavernous space.

The only other answer was the rapid clicking of leather soles against the cement floor. "The person is trying to get away. George, come on!"

In a flash Nancy took off across the hangar, toward the planes. She could hear George behind her, but she kept her attention focused on the footsteps coming from the maze of parked planes at the rear. She couldn't see the person, so Nancy could only dart around the planes. The footsteps sounded closer now.

She was only about twenty feet from the rear wall, when the footsteps fell silent. Nancy stopped short, motioning for George to do the same. They stood completely still, listening, but all Nancy heard were the raspy sounds of George's and her breathing.

"A person couldn't just disappear," George whispered.

"No way," Nancy whispered back.

A single row of six planes stood between them and the rear wall of the hangar. Bending low, Nancy peered into the semidarkness beneath the planes. Suddenly she saw a flash of olive green rushing toward the rear wall from behind a plane next to the one where she and George were standing. "There!" Nancy cried, pointing.

She and George raced forward, heading for the space between the planes and the rear wall. Just before they made it Nancy heard a door bang open. She caught a glimpse of an olive pants leg disappearing through a doorway in the rear wall.

"Oh, no, you don't," Nancy said under her breath. She pounded the last fifteen feet to the door, pulled it open, and ran outside. She whipped her head back and forth. "No one!" she cried, not bothering to hide her frustration.

George came up behind her, breathing hard. "Which way?"

"You go left. I'll go right," Nancy called. She took off, stopping to peer into the narrow lanes between the hangars. She was just passing the rear door of the last hangar in the row when it banged open. Nancy had to stop short to keep from smashing into the uniformed person who stepped into her path.

"Ensign Drew! What are you doing here?"

Nancy blinked in surprise at Rhonda Kisch, who was standing glaring at her. Nancy snapped to attention, frantically searching her mind for an explanation that wouldn't blow her cover. "I, uh, wanted to check out the layout of the east field, in order to, uh, be prepared when we fly from here in our familiarization sessions."

"If you make it to that part of your training," the On Wing said. "I suggest you concentrate on your current training—and steer clear of places where you don't have any business."

"Yes, sir." As the On Wing dismissed Nancy and turned away, Nancy glanced quickly at her blue uniform. Rhonda Kisch couldn't be the person she'd been chasing, but Nancy couldn't help wondering what she was doing here.

When Nancy got back to the original hangar, George was waiting outside. "Who was that?" she asked.

"My On Wing," Nancy replied. "I couldn't exactly interrogate her, but I'd like to ask the guard if he's seen her or anyone else anywhere near this hangar."

As she and George threaded their way back through the planes, Nancy spotted something on the cement floor. "Hey, look at this," she said.

She held up a page that had been ripped from a Naval Aviation Training Operation Standards manual.

"This page must have fallen out of the manual of whoever it was we just saw," Nancy said. She frowned down at the page. "A class of twenty trainees starts here every week, and we aren't going to be able to investigate every single trainee's manual for a missing page."

"Still, if any of the trainees acts suspiciously, I'll check their NATOPS manual to see if page" —Nancy paused to look at the bottom of the ripped-out sheet—"one twenty-eight is missing."

George nodded, then turned to Nancy with worried brown eyes. "You know, whoever that was must know that you're investigating Jill's death," she said soberly. "You'd better watch your back, Nan."

"Hello?" Nancy opened the screen door to 1025 Van Allen Drive, a two-story, stucco house located in the town of Davis, just a few minutes' drive from the base. "Is anyone home?"

She gazed into the front hall of the house where Jill Parker had lived. Mail, car keys, and cosmetics were scattered on a table against the wall. Through open doorways on either side of the foyer, Nancy could see a living room to the left and a dining room to the right. Stairs rose up from the foyer, and a hallway next to the stairs led to the rear of the house.

"Just a sec!" a woman's voice called from upstairs. A second later a young woman with dark-brown skin, short braids, and a warm smile jogged down the stairs. She was wearing cut-off sweats, an orange bathing suit top, and no shoes. She carried a NATOPS manual in one hand.

When she saw Nancy, she stopped on the stairs and smacked herself lightly on the forehead. "I completely forgot you were arriving today! Ensign Nancy Drew, right?"

When Nancy nodded, the woman came the rest of the way down the stairs and shook her hand. "Nice to meet you. I'm Yolanda Watts. I know I don't look like an ensign right now, but if I'm not comfortable while I study, nothing sinks in."

"I know what you mean," Nancy said, smiling.

"It only gets harder," Yolanda said. "Sometimes I think I must be crazy, but then I decide it's worth it to become a fighter pilot. I'm not sure where Diane and Mary are, but I'm sure you've had a long day. I'll show you where your room is so you can get settled and shower."

Nancy liked Yolanda's warm, open attitude. She followed her upstairs to a small room at the rear of the house. "Bathroom's halfway down the hall," Yolanda told her before disappearing into a room at the front of the house.

When Nancy came out of the shower twenty minutes later, she heard Yolanda talking to some other people downstairs. Sounds like my other roommates are here, she thought. After changing into baggy white shorts and a red T-shirt, she went down to the living room.

"Hi, Nancy," Yolanda called from the couch. "Come on in and meet the rest of the household."

Nancy saw that Mary Chambers was sitting on

a worn chair across from the couch, still wearing her zip-up coverall. "We've already met," Mary said flatly, forcing a smile.

The third girl in the room was sitting on the couch next to Yolanda. She was petite, with wavy, russet hair, a round face, and intelligent amber eyes. "Hi," she greeted Nancy with a wave. "I'm Diane Vega. If Mary seems a little out of it, you'll have to excuse her. Her plane almost crashed today."

"Yes, I know. I was there when it happened," Nancy said, coming into the room. Turning to Mary, she asked, "Do you know what was wrong with the computer controls yet?"

"No." Mary barely glanced at Nancy. Getting up from her chair, she headed for the stairs. "I'm going to shower and get some studying done. See you guys."

Again, Nancy found herself wondering why Mary was so reluctant to talk to her. And why did she seem so suspicious of Nancy? Was it possible that *she* was the person who had been eavesdropping on her and George?

"What if there's some kind of computer bug going around?" Yolanda asked, breaking into Nancy's thoughts. "First there were problems with the simulators, and now this. And after what happened to Jill . . ." She shivered, then said worriedly, "We could all be in danger every time we take a Mentor up."

"There were problems with the computer simulators?" Nancy asked, sitting in the chair Mary had vacated. She knew that part of the fighter pilot training consisted in using sophisticated computer graphics that re-created various flying conditions. It was a way to get used to maneuvering the T-34C in the more difficult spins and turns, without the danger of crashing.

Diane nodded. "I had to miss my session this afternoon because my simulator went on the fritz," she said.

"Jill had a lot of problems with the simulators, too," Yolanda added. "She told me she was going to make an official complaint."

"Oh, yeah?" Nancy wasn't sure what the problems with the simulators might have to do with Jill's death but she wanted to find out more about them. "I hope they get the kinks worked out before *I* start on the simulators. I'm psyched to do that part of my training. What's it like?"

Diane shrugged. "I rescheduled my session for tomorrow morning. You're welcome to tag along if you have the time."

"That'd be great," Nancy told her. Her stomach growled, reminding her that she hadn't eaten since that morning. "I'm starved! What do you guys usually do for dinner?" ,

"I'm too beat to cook," Yolanda said. "Anyone feel like heading to Wings? It's a restaurant in town," she explained to Nancy. "A lot of fighter pilot trainees go there."

"In other words, a lot of *guys* go there," Diane put in, grinning at Nancy. "So get ready to be asked out by half the male population of Davis."

Nancy laughed, then said, "If they're anything like the guy I saw giving Mary a hard time today, I think I'll pass on all of them."

"That was Crash Beauford," Diane said, rolling her eyes. "He thinks that just because there's a lot of navy brass in his family, he can say whatever he wants."

"There's stiff competition among trainees, but Crash goes way overboard—especially when it comes to women. Most of the guys here aren't nearly as obnoxious as he is," Yolanda told Nancy. "If we're lucky, Crash and his cronies won't even be there tonight."

Nancy remembered what Admiral Lewis had told her about Jill Parker being a top fighter pilot trainee. "Is Crash one of the top trainees in your class?"

"Actually, he's *the* top trainee, now that Jill's . . . gone," Diane answered.

Nancy couldn't help wondering about Crash. Would he go as far as committing murder to be at the top of his training class? It didn't seem likely, she thought, but decided to keep an eye on Crash Beauford.

Wings was an informal restaurant decorated with navy paraphernalia and framed photos of famous aircraft carriers. It was crowded with personnel from the base. Most were in jeans or shorts, but a few wore uniforms. Nancy guessed they had come directly from the base without changing. There was only a handful of other women besides her small group.

As they stepped past the bar, Diane pointed to a large group sitting at three tables that had been pushed together. "Looks like the new trainees," she commented. "Have you met them yet, Nancy?"

Nancy shook her head, eyeing the group. There were just two women at the table with the dozen or so men. They were all eating and talking animatedly. "I missed yesterday's class briefing," Nancy said, "and I was so busy today that I haven't had a chance to meet the rest of my class—"

She broke off as a loud male voice blared behind her. "Hey, Beauford! You must be happy."

Nancy turned around to see a beefy young man with a blond crewcut lean toward the dark-haired guy who had taunted Mary at the south airfield that afternoon. So the dark-haired guy was Crash Beauford, she thought, eyeing him. He was still wearing his mirrored sunglasses, even though he was inside. He was sitting with the same two guys she'd seen him with earlier.

"What's to be happy about, Taylor?" Crash asked.

"Jill Parker. You must be happy she's out of the competition," the blond guy taunted. "Because you know you'd never be top gun with her around."

Nancy couldn't believe the guy was speaking so callously about Jill so soon after her death. Crash's whole body tightened. He reached over and grabbed the blond guy by the shirt. "What did you say?"

"You heard me," Taylor said, swatting Crash's hand away.

The next thing Nancy knew, both men were stumbling toward her with their fists flying!

Chapter

Four

"HEY!" NANCY JUMPED to the side as Crash and the other guy moved toward her. She wedged herself against the wall next to the counter and just missed being hit by a right that Crash threw. Neither of the guys seemed to be aware of her—they were going at each other like a couple of wild animals. Half a dozen other people jumped on top of them, but Crash and Taylor had knocked over two tables before they were finally separated.

"You've got a lot to learn about Crash Beauford, pal," Crash shouted at the other guy. "Cross me and you'll live to regret it!" His sunglasses had fallen off, and he strained against his friends' arms, red-faced and disheveled. Nancy noticed a bruise over his left eye that was already starting to swell.

"I'm quaking in my boots, Beauford," Taylor shot back sarcastically. Taylor gave Crash a final scathing look, then shook himself free of the people holding him and stalked out of the restaurant.

Crash's friends didn't let him go until after the door closed and the other trainee was gone. "It's over, man. Calm down," a red-haired guy told Crash. Turning to the man behind the bar, he called, "Hey, Ernie! Can we get some ice over here?"

Nancy took a close look at Crash Beauford while he held an ice cube over the swelling cut. What was it he'd said? Cross me and you'll live to regret it? Maybe that was what Jill had done— crossed Crash by edging him out as top of their class.

She was jolted from her thoughts by the sudden realization that Crash Beauford was staring right at her. His smoldering, dark blue eyes were locked on hers, and Nancy found that she couldn't look away. As she took in the strong, square cut of his jaw—softened by a dimple in his chin—she felt an involuntary thrill run through her.

"Well, well, well . . ." Crash drew out the words, checking Nancy out from head to toe. A flirtatious smile played across his mouth as he sauntered over to her. "Who have we here?"

Nancy took a deep breath to quiet her racing pulse. "Ensign Nancy Drew. I just started the fighter pilot training program."

"Another little lady who wants to fly the Stealth bomber, eh? When are you girls going to learn that women belong in the kitchen, not in the cockpits of fighter planes?"

"And when are guys like you going to realize that we women can defend our country as well as any man, maybe better," Nancy shot back with a toss of her head. She wasn't flirting, she told herself, simply defending herself. "At least I don't lose my head every time I turn around."

"Oh, yeah? I think *I* could get you to lose your head, Ensign Nancy Drew."

The look Crash gave her was so electric that Nancy had to catch her breath. For a moment all she could do was stare into his magnetic blue eyes. Finally she managed to look away. She did a double take when her gaze flitted over his left wrist.

"Nice watch," she commented, keeping her voice casual. "Is it new?" He wore a metal watch, but the tan line on his wrist was wider than the watch's silver band. It looked to Nancy as if he had worn a different watch until recently— maybe until he'd left his other watch inside Jill Parker's plane?

Crash's gaze narrowed but only for a second. "Let me tell you something, Nancy. There's a lot more to know about Crash Beauford than just what kind of watch I wear," he said easily. "How'd you like to have dinner tomorrow night and—"

"Nancy! Over here!" Yolanda's voice called out from a table across the restaurant.

"I've got to go," Nancy told Crash, without answering his question. As she walked away, she felt his eyes boring into her back. She had to resist the urge to turn back. Despite his arrogance, she had to admit that Crash was attractive —dangerously attractive.

For the next hour Nancy pushed aside all thoughts of the case and enjoyed her blackened amberjack, a delicious local fish. When the meal was over, her housemates headed back home, but Nancy stayed behind to meet the trainees in her class.

"So you're the mysterious Ensign Drew," one of the two girls said after Nancy had introduced herself. "The rest of us were beginning to think that you were a figment of the navy's imagination."

"I had a personal emergency back home, so I arrived a day late," Nancy said. It wasn't a total lie. She'd needed the extra day's training with Gunnery Sergeant McDaniel.

Pulling over a chair from an empty table, Nancy sat at the end of the long table. The trainees in her class came from all over the country and had a variety of backgrounds. Nancy wished she had more time to get to know them, but she had a feeling her case was going to keep her pretty busy.

"I'm glad you found us," a guy named Greg told her. "We're having a barbecue and volleyball match at the beach this Sunday. Can you make it?"

"I'll be there," Nancy promised, smiling. Sunday was just two days away. She didn't know if she would know the truth about Jill's death by then, but hoped she'd be able to take a few hours off.

Nancy was about to leave when she saw George enter the restaurant with Richard Mirsky. George was wearing a sleeveless yellow- and white-striped dress with a white belt and white sandals. She hadn't exactly dressed up, but the outfit wasn't as casual as the jeans and T-shirts George usually wore. Judging from the easy way she and Richard were laughing and talking, they were getting along better than ever.

Nancy excused herself, saying she was going to the ladies' room. On her way she made a point of passing close to the table where George and Richard had just been seated. When George saw her, Nancy gestured for her to meet her in the ladies' room. As she stepped around the pay phone in the recessed area where the restrooms were, she glanced idly at the white-haired man on the phone. Her eyes flitted over his glasses and the bald spot on top of his head before she remembered where she'd seen him—on the stairs outside the admiral's office that afternoon.

"We're in big trouble on this one, Gary," the man was saying in hushed tones. "After what happened to the Parker girl, they're going over everything with a fine-tooth comb."

The Parker girl? It sounded as if he was talking about Jill! Nancy stopped short, peering at the man more closely. Even with his back to her, Nancy could tell he was distraught from the way he kept wiping his forehead with a white handkerchief.

"It doesn't look good for us," the man went on. A second later he turned in Nancy's direction and blinked at her, surprised. She started to push through the ladies' room door, but before she could, the man's eyes narrowed to slits. The icy expression in his pale eyes chilled Nancy to the bone.

If looks could kill, she thought, I would be a goner.

Chapter
Five

NANCY QUICKLY PUSHED through the ladies' room door and leaned against one of the sinks, her heart pounding. George was whistling to herself as she came in a few moments later.

"What's up?" George asked. Her smile faded when she saw Nancy's face. "Is something wrong?"

"I'm not sure," Nancy answered. "I just heard someone talking about Jill Parker and being in some kind of big trouble." She frowned, shaking her head. "It wasn't anything specific, but when the guy saw me, he seemed *very* unhappy that I'd overheard him."

"You mean that gray-haired guy on the phone?" George asked. When Nancy nodded, George continued, "That's Steven Eriksen. He's in charge of technical support for AeroTech, the company that supplies computer simulation programs and some of the computer components in the training planes. He came by Admiral Lewis's office this afternoon."

"Computer simulation, huh?" Nancy echoed. "The girls in my house were talking about problems with the computer simulators. They said that Jill was planning on making a complaint to the top brass before she died. After hearing this guy, I wonder if Eriksen or his company had something to do with Jill's death."

George let out a low whistle. "You mean, they might have intentionally killed her?"

"Or maybe their shoddy workmanship resulted in a problem with the computer controls in her plane," Nancy said, frowning. "Lieutenant Commander Styles didn't say anything about it in his report, but maybe they might have contributed to the crash. In any case, I'd like to find out more about AeroTech."

"Why don't you talk to Richard?" George suggested. "He told me that he interviewed Eriksen for his article."

Raising an eyebrow at George, Nancy said, "I don't want to barge in on your date—"

"Don't worry about it. It's not as if it's a *date* date," George said, turning away to study her reflection in the wide mirror above the sink. Nancy had a feeling George wasn't ready to talk about what was happening between her and Richard, so she changed the subject.

"The reason I wanted to talk to you is that I

was hoping you could take a look at some personnel files for me," Nancy said. She went on to tell George about her encounter with Crash Beauford. When she was done, George shook her head and said, "Wow. He sounds like a real loose cannon."

"Mmm." The image of Crash's dimpled chin and intense blue eyes popped into Nancy's head, and she had to force herself to concentrate. "Maybe it's just a coincidence that he has a new watch—or maybe he lost his old one while he was sabotaging Jill Parker's plane. In any case, I want to check him out more thoroughly." She paused for a moment, then added, "See what you can find out about Rhonda Kisch, my On Wing. And about Mary Chambers, too."

"The girl whose plane almost crashed today," George said, nodding. "So, Rhonda Kisch, Mary Chambers, and Crash . . . What's his last name again?"

"Beauford," Nancy supplied. She reached into her bag for the pencil and notepad she always carried, but pulled out a folded slip of paper instead. "That's funny—this wasn't in my bag before."

Nancy unfolded the paper and stared down at it in disbelief. In the middle of the page, typed in capital letters, were the words *BACK OFF—OR YOU WILL CRASH AND BURN*.

"Oh, no!" George said, peering over Nancy's shoulder. "Nancy, now we know for sure your cover's been blown!"

"Seems like it." Nancy frowned at her reflection in the mirror. "I'm almost convinced that Jill's death *wasn't* accidental, and that whoever's responsible doesn't want me to verify it."

She tapped a finger against the paper as she thought over the possibilities. "Rhonda saw us at the east airfield, but I haven't seen her since then. I don't see how she could have slipped me that note. I guess Crash could have found a way to put the note in my bag while I was eating. Or Mary could have done it before I left the house. We didn't find out who was sneaking around the hangar where Jill's plane is, so it could be almost anyone."

"I'm going to try to get a look at Crash's and Mary's NATOPS manuals. I have to start somewhere with someone. If either one is missing page one twenty-eight, that will give us more to go on."

"And I'll let you know if there's anything suspicious in any of the personnel files on the three you mentioned," George added. "The admiral gets to his office pretty early—before seven-thirty—so I'll be able to get on it first thing."

Nancy wrote down the three names for George, and then they left the ladies' room. The pay phone was no longer being used, Nancy noticed. "I don't see how Steven Eriksen could have slipped me that note, but I'd still like to hear whatever Richard can tell me about him and

AeroTech. You're sure you don't mind if I join you?"

George shook her head. "Positive. Anyway, I already told him about the case. Richard didn't even arrive at Davis Field until after Jill's plane crashed, so I figured it was okay."

Nancy felt uneasy about anyone else knowing their real reason for being at Davis Field. But if Richard could help them, it would be worth the risk. "It's fine," she assured George.

George led Nancy to the table where Richard was waiting. "Hi, there," he said, smiling at Nancy. His expression became sober, however, when she and George told him what Nancy had overheard Steven Eriksen say.

"Before I jump to any conclusions, I was hoping you could tell me what you know about AeroTech," Nancy finished.

Richard took a long drink of his soda, then rubbed his chin thoughtfully. "It's no secret that companies like AeroTech have taken a hard hit because of cuts in military spending," he began. "AeroTech has already closed two of its plants, and the rumor in the industry is that they might go bankrupt."

"Sounds like a desperate situation," Nancy commented.

"One that calls for desperate measures," Richard told her. "I think AeroTech might have tried to save money by cutting corners on computer simulators in one of their California plants.

Company officials said it was unintentional, but I'm not so sure."

Nancy leaned forward over the table, trying to fit this information into her case. "The other trainees in my house said there've been problems with the simulators here at Davis Field, as well."

"So maybe AeroTech has provided Davis with faulty equipment," George guessed.

"Today, Mary swore that she lost control of her plane because the computerized controls malfunctioned. AeroTech supplies those controls, right?" she asked Richard.

"Right." He looked back and forth between George and Nancy, a light of comprehension blinking on in his pale blue eyes. "You think AeroTech's shoddy workmanship might have caused Jill Parker's plane to malfunction, too?" When Nancy nodded, he let out a low whistle. "But if that's true—"

"Then AeroTech is responsible for Jill's death," George finished. "How could anyone put people's lives in jeopardy just to save a little money!"

Richard reached over and casually brushed a brown curl off George's forehead. "AeroTech is a multibillion-dollar industry, and the military accounts for most of their business," he pointed out. "They have a lot at stake." He frowned down at his plate a moment before adding, "Of course if they provide substandard equipment, AeroTech runs the risk of losing the navy's business anyway. Their contract with Davis Field expires in a few months. If word gets to Admiral Lewis that AeroTech's equipment isn't performing well, Steven Eriksen is going to have a hard time renewing his company's contract."

Nancy agreed, then snapped her fingers and sat bolt upright. "Jill was planning to make an official complaint about the computer simulators here at Davis, which could have tipped the scales so that Admiral Lewis would award the contract to another company."

"You think Eriksen sabotaged Jill's plane to keep her from making the complaint?" George asked, her mouth dropping open. "But he's a civilian. I doubt he has unlimited access to the base. How could he even get to the planes?"

"And again, if they sabotaged the computer controls, they'd run the risk of looking bad themselves and losing the navy's business anyway," Richard added.

"But if AeroTech sabotaged some *other* part of the plane, then the navy wouldn't suspect them," Nancy countered. "After all, Styles's report *did* state that engine failure caused the crash, and what I saw of the crash backs that up." Richard and George both opened their mouths, but Nancy held up a hand to stop them. "I know that still doesn't explain Mary's near accident," she said quickly. "I'm not sure what AeroTech's game is, but I definitely plan to check out Steven Eriksen."

"Eriksen has an office in Pensacola," Richard said. "I'm fairly sure AeroTech's office will be open tomorrow even though it's Saturday. I'll make an appointment with Steven to keep him at the base, so you can investigate."

"That'd be great," Nancy told him. Turning to George, she said, "Let's visit tomorrow after I finish FAM-One."

"Why don't I meet you two for dinner afterward?" Richard suggested, reaching over to touch George's arm.

George's brown eyes glistened with pleasure as she turned to Nancy. "What do you think?"

"Sounds good to me," Nancy said, not hesitating. Looking back and forth between Richard and George, she thought, It looks as if *something* good might come out of this case, after all.

"Nancy, there's a call for you!"

Nancy cracked open her eyes at the sound of Yolanda's voice outside her bedroom door the next morning. "Mmm," she said sleepily. "Be right there."

A quick glance at her travel clock told her that it was a few minutes after eight. Getting out of bed, Nancy put on her robe and went to the telephone, which was on a table in the upstairs hallway. "Hello?"

"Hi, it's me," George's voice came over the line. "I know you probably can't talk, but I wanted to tell you that Admiral Lewis got the report on Mary's plane."

Suddenly Nancy felt wide-awake. "And?"

"The computerized control contained a defective part," George told her. "Admiral Lewis hit the roof and woke Steven Eriksen to chew him out. He's going to make appointments to meet with other companies that supply computer components and simulation programs."

Nancy could hear Mary moving around inside her room, right next to the phone, so all she said was "I see. Thanks for calling me."

"Someone's there, eh?" George guessed. "We can talk more at the AeroTech's office later."

"Sounds good. 'Bye." It didn't seem possible that the company would intentionally sabotage Mary's plane—not when the malfunction could be traced to them so easily. It was more likely that the defective part was simply the result of the company's negligence.

She was still standing in the hallway when Diane called up the stairs, "Hey, Nancy! Are you ready to go? My session on the computer simulator starts at oh-nine hundred."

"I'll be there in a sec!" she called back. She hadn't meant to sleep so late, but she'd been thinking about the case and hadn't been able to fall asleep until after one o'clock. Nancy flew to the bathroom to wash her face, then hurriedly dressed in her olive flight uniform before grabbing her NATOPS manual and running downstairs to meet Diane. "Sorry," she said.

Diane was also wearing her coverall, her russet hair tucked beneath her cap. "No harm done.

We'll still get there on time," she told Nancy. "Why don't you follow me in your car, so we can go our separate ways afterward?"

Twenty minutes later Nancy pulled her car to a stop next to Diane's hatchback in front of a building not far from the administration bloc. A sign over the entrance read Training.

Inside, they passed through a common area with mailboxes, a bulletin board, and a few worn-looking couches and chairs. Diane led the way down a long hallway and through a doorway marked Simulators.

The spacious, open room contained what looked like half a dozen planes that had been stripped of their wings and tails. All that remained of each plane was a cockpit bolted to a metal base on the floor. From what Nancy could see, the controls were identical to the controls of the T-34C. But instead of a windshield, each simulator had a computer screen. A guy was sitting in the cockpit of the nearest simulator. Looking at the computer screen, she had the feeling of being inside a plane.

"It's impressive, isn't it?" Diane asked, following Nancy's gaze. "Come on, let's get settled and I'll show you what these things are all about."

After signing her name in the logbook by the door, Diane went to Simulator 5, at the far end of the room. Next to the simulator, a dark-haired man in a lieutenant's uniform was talking to a gray-haired man in civilian clothes. "That's my instructor, Vic Santana," Diane told Nancy in a low voice, nodding toward the lieutenant. As the two girls approached, they saluted Lieutenant Santana. "Sir, this is Ensign Drew, one of the new trainees," Diane said, nodding toward Nancy. "She'd like to see a simulator. Mind if I give her a demonstration?"

"Not at all," the lieutenant replied easily, but Nancy barely heard him. She was too busy staring at the gray-haired man. It was Steven Eriksen! He did a double take when he saw Nancy.

"This is Steven Eriksen. He's in charge of technical support for AeroTech," Lieutenant Santana went on. "He's keeping an eye on things to make sure they run smoothly."

Eriksen smiled, but his eyes remained cool. While Diane climbed into the simulator's cockpit and strapped on her safety harness, Eriksen gave a curt nod and walked away.

Diane turned to Nancy who was standing behind her and said, "The computer programs re-create the airspace we fly in around Davis Field. Today I'm going to be flying from the south airfield. So when I take off and maneuver the plane, the computer graphics will simulate what I'd be seeing if I were really flying there."

"I view the same graphics on a second console, here," Lieutenant Santana said to Nancy. He pointed to a video screen set up in front of a chair outside the cockpit. "That way I can review Diane's performance."

Diane flipped a switch, and the view from the south airfield popped onto the screen. Nancy felt as if she were really looking at the palm trees and scrub oak that edged the field. As Diane pressed the controls to take off, the image on the screen angled up sharply so that there was nothing but sky. "I'm doing a series of spins today," Diane murmured. She kept her attention focused on the screen, her fingers moving confidently over the controls. "Banking right," she said.

A sudden sputtering noise came from the screen, making Nancy blink. "Look at that smoke," she said. "Is that normal?"

Dark puffs were coming from the top of the screen, and they were letting off an acrid, burned smell. Diane's eyes flicked away from the graphics, and she frowned. "Hey! What's going on?"

Lieutenant Santana jumped up from his console. Out of the corner of her eye, Nancy saw Steven Eriksen approach, too. As the two men moved up beside her, she heard a series of loud electrical popping noises from behind the screen.

Nancy gasped in horror. "I think it's going to blow—"

Her words were cut off by a loud *boom!* as the entire computer screen shattered!

Chapter

Six

Nancy THREW HERSELF BACKWARD as hot shards of glass and plastic were blown out from the screen with amazing force. She threw her hands up to protect her face, but not before a stinging sensation on her cheek made her wince. A cloud of smoke surrounded the simulator's cockpit, blackening Nancy's lungs. Even through the dark cloud, she could see a hot orange glow.

"It's burning! Diane, get out of the cockpit!" Nancy said urgently, coughing.

Nancy and Lieutenant Santana grabbed Diane's arms and helped her to scramble out. As they cleared the simulator a stream of pressurized white foam shot over Nancy's shoulder at the cockpit. Nancy saw that Steven Eriksen was using the fire extinguisher.

"Are you two all right?" he asked once he was

sure the fire was out. Behind his glasses, the expression in his eyes was tense and fearful.

Nancy felt the sticky ooze of blood dripping from the cut on her cheek. "I'm fine. I don't think my cut's serious," she answered, wiping at her face.

Diane was gingerly checking some minor cuts on her forehead and arms. "How do you like that? I've been wounded in action already, and we're not even in a war," she said with a shaky smile.

Maybe not an official one, Nancy thought. But a dangerous enemy is at work here anyway. While Lieutenant Santana waved the other trainees back to work, Nancy turned to Steven Eriksen and asked, "What happened?"

Eriksen wiped the sweat from his forehead before answering Nancy's question. "I'm going to make a complete inspection. You ladies can rest assured that nothing like this will happen again," he said, but Nancy didn't think even *he* was convinced by his words. "Why don't you two get those cuts taken care of. Then I'll set you up at Simulator Six."

Nancy and Diane washed up and got bandages at the first-aid station. When they returned to the simulators, Lieutenant Santana was already waiting at Simulator 6. Diane joined him, but Nancy couldn't resist pausing at Simulator 5. Steven Eriksen had removed some of the computer components from the damaged simulator and was sitting on the floor, inspecting one component in his hands. Judging by the concerned expression on his face, he didn't like what he was seeing.

"Everything okay?" Nancy asked, squatting down next to him.

"What?" Eriksen glowered at Nancy. She tried to get a look at the flat, three-inch-square component he was holding, but he slipped it into his pocket. "Everything's under control. Simulator Six is ready for you," he said, rising to his feet, in a hurry to get her out of the way.

"Hey, look at that," Nancy murmured to herself. Her eyes had focused on something blue that lay under the console where Diane had been sitting. She bent to look at it and saw that it was part of a sheet of bright blue notepaper. Nancy could see a few letters of back-slanted handwriting, but most of the paper had been burned—she couldn't make out any of the words.

The explosion had blown most of the mess to the rear of the simulator, but this paper was *at the front* of the simulator. She hadn't noticed the paper previously, but before she could pick it up, Steven Eriksen said firmly, "Lieutenant Santana is waiting."

He quickly ushered Nancy to the adjoining simulator, but Nancy saw his eyes flick nervously back toward the piece of blue paper. What could be so important about that piece of paper that he kept looking at it as if it were part of a recurring nightmare?

Nancy didn't know what AeroTech's technical

support director was up to, but she definitely planned to find out.

"'Bye, Diane. Thanks for letting me tag along."

"No problem. At least we didn't have another explosion," Diane told her. "I've got to run to get to the south airfield for FAM-Nine. See you."

Nancy walked over to the bank of phones on the wall at the far end of the training lounge. Nancy decided to call Admiral Lewis's office to tell him about her theory that Jill's death might be related to the problems with the simulators. In addition to three pay phones, there were two phones for making calls within the base. Nancy used one of those and dialed the admiral's extension. His secretary picked up, then put George on.

"Hi, Nan. What's up?" George greeted her. When Nancy told her about the explosion on the computer simulator, George exclaimed, "Are you sure you're all right?"

"Positive," Nancy assured her. "I think Steven Eriksen tried to hide something about the explosion. He pocketed one of the components when I tried to look at it. Admiral Lewis should make sure someone else examines the part."

"I'll tell him about it," George promised. "Anyway, I'm glad you called. I just finished going through the personnel files for Crash Beauford, Rhonda Kisch, and Mary Chambers."

She paused before adding, "It was pretty interesting reading."

Nancy gripped the telephone receiver more tightly. "You found something to implicate one of them?" she asked.

"I didn't find anything unusual on Rhonda Kisch. She's a navy brat who followed in her dad's footsteps. Did well at the Naval Academy; has a flawless record. Crash Beauford's another story, though. He got a college degree from some school in Louisiana before he enlisted in the navy. Guess what he majored in?"

"Sabotage and all-around sneakiness?"

"Close," George said, laughing. "He studied computer engineering."

Nancy let out her breath in a rush. "Wow. So if someone *did* tamper with Jill's plane's computer, Crash is a likely candidate because he wanted to be top gun," she said. "Of course, that still doesn't explain why he would tamper with the simulators. Or why he would mess with the computer controls of Mary's training plane. By the way, was there anything unusual in *her* file?"

"One thing," George answered. "I'm not sure if it means anything, but Mary Chambers and Jill Parker both came from the same town. Some place in Kentucky called Ventura."

"Hmm," Nancy said. "There could be something between the two of them."

"Something that would make Mary *kill* Jill?" George sounded dubious. "I don't know, Nan.

Mary's plane was sabotaged, too. And that watch we found was a man's."

"I know it's a long shot. It's just something to keep in mind, that's all," Nancy said. She turned as the door to the lounge opened and Rhonda Kisch walked in in uniform. She gave Nancy a critical glance before stepping over to the mailboxes and slipping an envelope into one of them. "I have to go," Nancy said to George, lowering her voice. "Meet me at the south airfield at four o'clock. That's when my flight session ends."

"Sixteen hundred hours?" George said. "Aye, aye, Ensign. See you then." Nancy could practically see George's teasing salute. She chuckled to herself as she hung up the phone.

"Good morning, Ensign. Nice to know that you have time to slack off."

Nancy groaned inwardly when she saw that Lieutenant Kisch was standing right next to her. Nancy gave a salute and said, "Sir! I wasn't slacking off. I was just—"

"We'll see about that this afternoon, Ensign," Rhonda Kisch said, cutting her off. She tapped Nancy's NATOPS manual, which was on the shelf beneath the phone she had been using. "You have to know this thing inside out if you're going to succeed as a fighter pilot."

"Yes, sir," Nancy said, trying to ignore the sinking sensation in the pit of her stomach. She hadn't had a chance to even glance at the material she was supposed to know for FAM-1, and she knew her On Wing wouldn't cut her any slack.

"See you at thirteen hundred hours, Ensign." Lieutenant Kisch gave Nancy a quick salute, then left.

Nancy would have liked to talk to Kisch to find out what, if anything, the lieutenant knew about Jill Parker's death. But an ensign couldn't interrogate a superior officer. Stifling her frustration, Nancy tried to think of the leads that *were* open to her. She still had an hour and a half before her flight session. She and George would be visiting Steven Eriksen's office later that day, and Nancy figured she'd have the opportunity to check out Mary Chambers at their house. But she knew Crash wasn't going to be easy to investigate. She had to try, though.

Nancy's gaze fell on a plastic-bound directory hanging by a chain from one of the phones. Nancy turned to the *B*'s and ran her finger down the page until she got to Beauford. "Beauford, Eddie," she murmured. He was the only Beauford in the directory—it had to be Crash. Nancy memorized the address, then looked it up on a map of the area. She just hoped that he *and* his roommates wouldn't be home!

When she pulled up across the street from the weathered, two-story wooden house where Crash lived, the hot sun was high in the sky and a warm sea breeze was blowing in off the Gulf. Nancy was relieved to see that there were no cars in front of the house. After jogging to the front door, she knocked, just to be safe.

Good, she thought. No answer. She tried the

door, grinning to herself when she found it wasn't locked. "So far, so good," she murmured.

The front door opened directly into the living room. Sneakers and clothes were scattered across the worn furniture and on the woven straw mat covering the floor. At the rear of the room a flight of stairs led up. Nancy took a step toward them, then stopped and cocked her head to one side.

Was that a noise she'd heard upstairs? "Hello?" she called tentatively, but there was no answer. Must have been the wind blowing, she decided. Moving quietly, Nancy took the stairs to the second floor and peeked inside the rooms lining the upstairs hall. In the second bedroom, she saw a desk against the far wall, next to an open closet. On the desk was a photograph of Crash with an older couple Nancy guessed were his parents. Next to the photo was a red visor exactly like the one she'd seen Crash wear earlier. It was on top of a NATOPS manual.

Now I'm in business, Nancy thought. If that manual is missing page 128, then Crash is the person who was eavesdropping on George and me when we were examining Jill Parker's plane.

As she started toward the desk something else caught her eye—a piece of bright blue paper sticking out from the pages of the manual. It was covered with back-slanted handwriting. A jolt of adrenaline shot through Nancy. "Whoa! That looks like—"

She broke off, hearing the scrape of a shoe on

the floor behind her. Before she could turn around, two hands shoved her.

"Hey!" Nancy flew forward into the open closet. A split second later the closet door slammed shut, and she heard the click of a lock.

She was shut in!

Chapter

Seven

NANCY CAUGHT HER ARMS in a tangle of hanging shirts and had to tug them free before she could pound on the door.

"Let me out!" she yelled. She pressed her ear to the closet door, but all she heard was the sound of footsteps running away. Was it Crash? But then, why would he run away? After all, *she* was the one sneaking around.

"This is great," she muttered grimly into the darkness. In the closed, stuffy space, it felt twenty degrees hotter than the rest of the house. Beads of sweat sprang out on her forehead, and others dripped down her legs. Dropping down on her heels, Nancy felt around the doorknob, trying to gauge what kind of lock the door had. There was no keyhole, but when she touched the knob itself, she felt a small hole at its center.

Great! She'd had experience with this kind of lock. The mechanism to spring the lock was inside the doorknob. If she could maneuver something into the hole and twist it exactly right . . .

"I know," she whispered to herself. She pulled out one of the bobby pins she'd used in her French braid that morning. After unbending the metal pin, she stuck it into the hole and probed around. She had been poking around for only a few moments when she heard a door bang open somewhere inside the house.

Nancy's body went taut. Someone was there! She didn't know if it was the same person who'd locked her in, or someone else, but in either case she didn't want to be caught inside the closet. "Come on . . ." she urged under her breath. She heard footsteps thumping up the stairs now. In just a few seconds more, the person would be up there.

"Yes!" she whispered triumphantly as the lock clicked open. In a flash, she turned the knob, pushed open the door, and jumped out of the closet. Now, if she could just find a way out of here before . . .

"Hey! What are you doing in here?"

Nancy's heart leapt into her throat when she saw Crash Beauford standing in the door frame. His expression was tense, and the little muscle above his jawbone moved rhythmically in and out. As he strode into the room, Nancy took an involuntary step backward.

"Crash! I, uh—I'm really happy I found you!" she said, flashing him a big smile.

A slow smile played over Crash's lips, deepening the dimple in his chin. "Are you?" He sauntered closer, fixing her with his intense gaze. "Because if I didn't know better, I'd say that I'd just caught you snooping."

Nancy's pulse was racing a mile a minute. As he came closer and closer, she felt a charged current bounce between them. "No! I— That's not it at all—" She tried to back away from him, but Crash's desk blocked her retreat.

"What *is* it, then? Don't tell me you came all the way here to tell me I'm the most irresistible guy you've ever met?" Crash asked, his voice a slow, seductive drawl. He was just inches from her now, his powerful frame blocking her path to the door. "Don't toy with me, Ensign Nancy Drew. You'll get more than you bargained for."

His blue eyes seemed to bore right through her, and a tingle went down Nancy's spine. She noticed his eyelashes, long and sooty, slowly brush his tanned cheekbones. Gazing at her below heavy lids, he bent closer.

Before Nancy could even think about what to do, his lips hovered over hers, and he gave her a playful smile. A small voice in the back of her head told her to push him away, but somehow she couldn't. His lips drew closer, and she felt the heat from his skin. He was so handsome! Despite herself, she lifted her face to his. He kissed her—a steamy kiss—holding her tight against his muscular chest. A long moment passed before he finally pulled away.

"Now, what are you *really* doing here, Nancy?" Crash whispered.

Nancy put a hand on his desk to steady herself, then blinked as she took in Crash's NATOPS manual. Get a grip, Drew! she ordered herself. You're here on a case, remember?

She shook herself, then turned and tapped Crash's manual. "Actually, I was wondering if I could, uh, borrow your NATOPS manual to photocopy a page that's missing from mine," she fibbed. "I was at the beach, so I thought I'd stop by."

Crash's gaze flew to his desk, where his NATOPS manual sat, and his whole expression changed. His eyes narrowed, and his jaw became set again. Reaching past Nancy, he picked up the manual and tucked it under his arm. "Sorry, but I've got to study all afternoon," he said guardedly. Then he raised a dark eyebrow and added, "I can see right through you, Nancy."

"You can?" she asked, trying to keep the nervousness from her voice.

Crash let out a deep laugh. "Sure. Listen, if you want to go out with me, why don't you just come out and ask? You don't have to make all these excuses." As he spoke, Crash took her arm and led her from the room. She didn't have any choice but to let herself be ushered down the stairs. She tried to get a look at the blue paper she'd seen, but it was out of sight beneath Crash's arm. "So let's plan on dinner for two tonight," he went on. "It'll be an experience you'll never forget."

I'll bet, Nancy thought. She couldn't tell if he was serious, or just playing some kind of dangerous game with her. "I have plans," Nancy said, without meeting his gaze.

"Too bad. Maybe another time."

"Mmm." After saying goodbye, Nancy returned to her convertible, where she sat trying to collect her thoughts.

Whoa! What just happened? There weren't many guys who had the kind of effect on her that Crash Beauford did. And what was worse, Crash *knew* she was attracted to him. Nancy wasn't sure why she'd kissed him, but she knew she was going to have to be *very* careful around him from now on.

"So Crash caught you in his room, huh?" George looked up from her desk, worriedly. "You'd better be careful, Nan. If Crash sabotaged Jill's plane, he's not going to be happy about your digging up dirt on him."

"Mmm." After returning to the base, Nancy had stopped by the admiral's office to fill George in on what had happened at Crash's. They were both speaking in whispers, so as not to disturb the admiral's secretary. Nancy had decided not to say anything about Crash kissing her. She didn't want George to worry about her more than she already was. Besides, no matter how thrilling his kiss may have been, there was no way Nancy was going to let Crash Beauford catch her off guard again. "I can't back off, though," Nancy went on. "There are too many unanswered questions."

"Like, if Crash wasn't the person who locked you in his closet, then who was?" George supplied.

"And why would someone else be sneaking around his house?" Nancy added. "Anyway, I only have a few minutes before I have to meet Rhonda Kisch at the south field. Did Admiral Lewis get a report on the accident at the computer simulator yet?"

George glanced at the closed door to the admiral's office. "He had a conference call with Steven Eriksen and some big cheese from AeroTech's home office, but I'm not sure what they talked about."

At that moment the door to the inner office opened and Admiral Lewis stuck his head out. "Fran, I've got a meeting with the defense secretary in Washington next month," he told his secretary. "I'll need you to make travel arrangements . . ." His voice trailed off when he saw Nancy at George's desk. Nancy immediately saluted. After returning the salute, the admiral said, "Afternoon, Ensign. Could I have a word with you and Miss Fayne?"

"Yes, sir," Nancy replied. She and George both hurried into his office.

"I was sorry to hear about the accident at the

computer simulator this morning," he began after sitting at his desk. "How are you feeling?"

Nancy automatically reached up to touch the bandage on her cheek. "Fine," she told him. "Did you find out what caused the explosion?"

The admiral laced his fingers together on his desk and frowned. "The simulator contained a defective component, but Mr. Eriksen says the part wasn't made by his company. He claims that someone replaced AeroTech's component with a faulty one."

"Sounds like a half-baked excuse to cover up AeroTech's shoddy work," George commented, shaking her head.

"The same thought crossed my mind," Admiral Lewis said. "It makes me think that maybe AeroTech did sabotage Jill's plane to keep her from exposing—" The admiral broke off as the intercom on his desk buzzed. "Yes, Fran. What is it?"

"Bob Olmstead of Howard Technologies is here to see you, Admiral," the secretary's voice came through.

"I'll be out in a minute." Admiral Lewis clicked off. "I'm afraid you'll have to excuse me. Under the circumstances, I decided to get proposals for computer simulation programs from some other companies."

He stood up, and Nancy and George started toward the door. After promising to keep him up-to-date on the investigation, the two girls returned to the outer office. A rotund, red-faced man was sitting in a chair next to Fran's desk. He wore a blue suit and white shirt, and his dark hair was neatly slicked back. He was so busy studying the clipboard in his lap that he didn't seem to notice Nancy and George.

"See you later, George," Nancy said in a low voice. She waved casually, then jumped when she saw the clock on George's desk. "Yikes! It's already thirteen hundred hours. By the time I get to the south airfield, I'll be at least ten minutes late. My On Wing is going to kill me!"

Rhonda Kisch's eyes burned into Nancy's like laser beams. The lieutenant was furious that Nancy had shown up fifteen minutes late for FAM-1. She chewed Nancy out for being irresponsible, then began to pelt her with questions. They had been standing outside the hangar the whole time. Blistering sunshine beat down on them, and heat waves rose up from the runway, making it hard for Nancy to concentrate. So far, Nancy had managed to get all of the answers right, but Lieutenant Kisch still wasn't showing any signs of warming up to her.

Nancy couldn't help wondering if Rhonda had a special reason for being so hard on her—to keep her from investigating Jill's death, for instance. George had said that the lieutenant's record was spotless, though. Maybe being strict was just a part of her nature.

"Talk me through course rules, Ensign," the lieutenant next ordered.

During her crash-course preparation with Sergeant McDaniel, Nancy had learned that the navy had a specific training course for each of its three airfields at Davis Field. "Course rules" detailed the route and the altitude pilots were supposed to follow. Nancy had managed to get a quick look at the course for the south field in her NATOPS manual. Taking a deep breath, she tried to remember it.

"Take off south-southwest from the south field's airstrip—angle thirty degrees south—power up to one hundred seventy knots at thirteen hundred feet . . ." As she spoke, Nancy was relieved to find that she could picture the diagram of the route from the manual. Ten minutes later, when she finished describing the course, she was pretty sure she'd remembered it correctly. For a long moment Rhonda Kisch didn't say anything. When she finally spoke, all she said was "I guess you're as ready to take up the Mentor as you'll ever be."

It wasn't exactly glowing praise, but Nancy was happy to be starting flying. Rhonda led her over to one of the T-34C planes. The number 2378 was stenciled on the outside of the plane. "This Mentor is going to be yours and only yours for the duration of your training," Rhonda told her.

Nancy felt a thrill as she signed out the plane in the logbook, then went through the preflight check with Lieutenant Kisch. Finally she climbed into the Mentor's front position. She'd flown ordinary planes hundreds of times, but she knew the Mentor flew much faster and was capable of many more sophisticated and complicated maneuvers. While Rhonda took the rear position, Nancy checked over her control panel. After the grilling her On Wing had given her, Nancy already felt familiar with the T-34C. A buzz of excitement pulsed through her as she strapped herself into her safety harness and slipped on her helmet, which contained a headset and microphone.

Following Lieutenant Kisch's orders, Nancy started the plane's engine and taxied to the runway. Her On Wing gave the okay to take off, and Nancy started the Mentor speeding down the runway. Seconds later she eased the plane's nose up and felt a sensation of power and weightlessness that made her feel giddy. As she banked south, following course rules, she hit the buttons to retract the plane's landing gear, then checked her altitude and pressure gauges.

Nancy pushed her speed up to a hundred and seventy knots, which she knew was over two hundred miles an hour. It was the standard cruising speed for navy aircraft, more than twice as fast as most pilots flew in civilian planes.

"We won't be doing anything fancy the first time up, Ensign," Lieutenant Kisch's voice came through Nancy's earphones.

"Yes, sir," Nancy replied. As she pulled the Mentor in a wide turn to the east, she marveled at the power and precision of the T-34C. For the next hour and a half, Nancy followed the south airfield's standard course. She performed basic turns in every direction and flew the plane at various altitudes and speeds. Fancy spins and turns would come in later FAM sessions.

"Make your break now, Ensign," Lieutenant Kisch ordered as Nancy neared the south field at the end of her flight.

Nancy immediately responded to the order to break, which meant to prepare for her landing. In order to do that, she had to fly over the base from the water, then turn around and head back to the south airfield before touching down. After she passed over the cluster of Davis Field's compounds, she pulled the Mentor around in a hard turn and dropped her power to one hundred and fifty knots. Now she was heading south toward the airfield's landing strip. "Dropping landing gear . . ." she murmured into her microphone.

She was just hitting the proper controls when the Mentor suddenly began to shudder and cough. "Hey!" she cried. "Something's wrong with the engine—"

"What's the problem, Ensign?" Rhonda's voice came over the earphones. "Check your instruments."

Nancy's eyes had already flown to the gauges on the control panel in front of her. She gasped when she saw that the needle of her pressure gauge had dropped almost to zero. "My fuel pressure's shot!" she yelled into her microphone.

The plane was losing speed and altitude every second. Nancy's whole body tensed as the engine gave a final shudder, then died. "Oh, no!" she said on a single breath.

"Fuel's out." Her On Wing's tension-filled voice came over the headphones.

Nancy felt dread twist her stomach into knots as the plane dropped closer to the ground. Looking through the cockpit windows, she saw the base's solid, plain buildings up ahead.

Unless there's a miracle, Nancy thought, we're going to crash right into one of those buildings!

Chapter

Eight

W E'LL NEVER MAKE IT to the landing strip!" Nancy spoke into her microphone to her On Wing.

"Never say never, Ensign. Prepare for a dead-engine landing."

Lieutenant Kisch's calm voice helped to soothe Nancy. "Yes, sir." Nancy knew from previous flying experience that the plane's aero-dynamic design would keep it from spiraling nose-first into the ground—as long as she flew flawlessly. "I have to make sure my nose stays just above the horizon, right?"

"Right. But not too far above, or the wings will fail to buoy us up," the lieutenant said. "And no sharp turns—that'll throw off the balance."

The next few minutes were the most harrowing of Nancy's life. The plane angled dangerously low, just over the tops of the naval air station's buildings. Just when she thought they would surely hit one of them, the buildings were behind her. The south field was to her right, but Nancy didn't dare turn that sharply. She saw an open area directly in front of her.

"I'll have to touch down on that sandy field," she said tensely. She flicked on her landing lights and moments later felt the wheels fall into place. They hit and bumped over the uneven surface. Nancy managed to throw the switches to brake the Mentor. Several hundred yards later the plane finally came to a stop. For a long moment all she could do was sit and be thankful that she, Rhonda, and the T-34C had all made it through in one piece.

"Nice landing, Ensign," Rhonda Kisch's voice came through the headset. Nancy couldn't be sure, but she thought she heard a hint of respect in her On Wing's voice.

Nancy pulled off her helmet and turned to give her On Wing a shaky smile. "Thank you, sir. I don't know what the problem was. I had a full supply of fuel when I checked before takeoff."

Lieutenant Kisch unstrapped her safety harness and took off her helmet. "Let's take a look."

She and Nancy climbed out of the plane and pulled open the metal panel in front of the cockpit, where the engine and fuel lines were located. With her On Wing watching, Nancy went through the list of checks the navy required to make sure an aircraft was in good flying condition. After examining the engine, she moved on to the fuel line, starting at the point where it led in from the tank. The engine was still hot, but even without getting too close, Nancy could see the small puddles of fuel that had collected at the bottom of the plane beneath the fuel line.

"Sir, I think there's a leak here," she told Lieutenant Kisch. "But I'm sure it wasn't leaking before we took off."

The On Wing frowned down at the oily puddles. "It's possible that a weak spot in the fuel line started to leak after we were in the air."

Nancy barely heard her. Her attention was focused on the grease-covered fuel line. Because of the extreme heat, she couldn't touch it, but she thought she detected a clean rip in the line. "Sir? Wouldn't a leak from stress result in a ragged break?"

The lieutenant's frown deepened, but she said nothing. Nancy was beginning to feel as if her suspicions of the On Wing were misplaced. After all, she would hardly sabotage a plane that she knew she herself would be in.

It was only when they both heard an approaching Jeep that Rhonda turned to look at Nancy. "We're done for today, Ensign. I'll take it from here."

Nancy wanted to object, but her On Wing's stern attitude warned her to keep quiet. "Yes, sir."

The Jeep pulled up, and two young men in

trainees' coveralls jumped out. After Nancy and Rhonda assured them that they were okay, they drove Nancy back to the south airfield. When she got to the hangar, it was three forty-five. Good, Nancy thought. That gives me fifteen minutes to check out a few things.

At the logbook to the left of the hangar entrance, she ran her finger down the list of names. Each person who came into the hangar had to write down their time in and out, as well as the ID number of any planes taken out or worked on.

"Eddie Beauford," Nancy murmured, stopping her finger next to his name. He had signed in at eight-thirty that morning and out at eleven-thirty. That was about the amount of time each FAM session lasted.

Skimming down the rest of the names, Nancy saw that Mary Chambers had also been flying. She had arrived just after noon and had left at three-thirty.

"Hi, Nancy," a guy's voice spoke up next to her. Nancy turned to see Greg, a guy in her training class, standing at her elbow. "I saw that landing you just made. Way to go," he told her, giving her a thumbs-up.

"I was lucky," Nancy said. Then, looking at him more closely, she asked, "Have you been here long?" She didn't think Greg was involved in her case, but if he'd been in the hangar, perhaps he'd seen someone working on her plane. Unfortunately, he had arrived at the south airfield just as her plane was coming down.

Nancy talked to a few more trainees who were at the hangar, but they had been so involved with their own flight training that none of them had noticed anyone near her plane. When she went to meet George at her car, which was parked outside the hangar, she hadn't learned anything that might help her identify the saboteur.

George was leaning against the white convertible when Nancy got there. "How'd your flying session go?" George asked.

"I'll tell you about it while we drive to Pensacola," Nancy told her. "Did you get AeroTech's address from Richard?"

George nodded. The two girls got in the convertible, and while Nancy drove toward the exit from Davis Field she told George about the leak in her fuel line. "The cut looked too clean to have been caused by stress," she finished. "I'm pretty sure someone sabotaged it."

"Nancy, this is serious!" George exclaimed. "I guess whoever wrote you that note about crashing and burning meant it."

"I've been thinking about that. The note might not have been a threat. Maybe it came from someone who wanted to *warn* me about danger," Nancy said.

George shrugged, letting the wind ruffle her dark curls. "Hopefully, we'll have more to go on after we visit AeroTech."

Ten minutes later the girls crossed a bridge over Pensacola Bay and entered the city. Nancy followed the directions Richard Mirsky had given to the parking lot of an old brick building that looked as if it had once been some kind of factory. Now offices and stores occupied the building. Nancy looked over the series of doorways set into the brick, then pointed to one near the center of the building. "There it is—AeroTech," she said, reading the sign above the door.

"What's our plan?" George asked.

Nancy frowned toward the office's entrance. "There shouldn't be many people around, so if you'll just get Eriksen's secretary out of my way, I can sneak into his office and check it out."

Nancy went with George to AeroTech's door, then waited outside while George went in. She stood back from the glass door so she wouldn't be noticeable from inside the office, but she could still see into the reception area. A young woman sat behind a sleek counter. Behind her, Nancy could see a hallway with a few doors leading off it. Nancy watched furtively while George approached the secretary. A moment later the young woman led her down the hallway and into the first room. Before George disappeared inside, she turned and gave Nancy a quick thumbs-up. Then the door closed behind her.

"Here goes nothing—" Taking a deep breath, Nancy moved inside. The carpeting muffled the noise of her shoes as she slipped past the reception desk and started down the hallway. She paused outside the first doorway just long enough to hear George's voice through the closed door:

"I just need to see the repair records on every simulator AeroTech has supplied in the last three years."

Way to go, George! That ought to keep Eriksen's secretary busy for a while. Grinning to herself, Nancy hurried farther down the hall. The second door was partially open, and a plaque on it read Steven Eriksen. A quick glimpse told Nancy the office was empty, so she stepped inside and closed the door behind her. The office was just large enough to hold a filing cabinet and a desk piled with papers. She hoped that it wouldn't take long to search it.

Stepping over to the desk, Nancy sifted through the jumble of papers. There were descriptions of sophisticated computer simulators and graphs with projected costs. Nancy didn't find anything about the accidents on the computer equipment.

Opening the desk's top drawer, she found only stationery, pens, and other supplies, so she pushed it closed again and tried the file drawer below. She tugged on the drawer, but it was locked. It took only a second for Nancy to jimmy the lock with a bobby pin. When she pulled open the file drawer, the label on the first folder caught her attention right away: Press Clips—Negative PR.

"Bingo," she whispered. Plucking the file from the drawer, she opened it. There was a pile of articles that had been clipped from newspapers and magazines. Some speculated that military cutbacks had placed AeroTech on shaky financial ground. A series of articles from a southern California newspaper broke the story of Aero-Tech's defective equipment being used in a military base there. That had to be the same story Richard Mirsky had mentioned, Nancy realized.

"According to inside sources," Nancy read, "substandard workmanship was purposely over-looked by AeroTech's technical supervisor . . ." She did a double take when she read the name: "Steven Eriksen."

The article went on to say that while his guilt was never proven, Steven Eriksen's transfer from the California plant suggested that he was guilty. Nancy let out a low whistle. Richard hadn't mentioned that Eriksen had been tied to the California scandal. If Eriksen *had* allowed sub-standard parts to be delivered to the southern California military base, it was all the more likely that he was doing the same thing at Davis Field. All she had to do now was—

Nancy jolted upright as she heard the secretary's voice right outside her office door: "I'll get that for you right away, Ms. Fayne."

A second later the doorknob rattled. The re-ceptionist was coming into the office! Nancy checked frantically, but didn't see anywhere she could hide. In a second she was going to be caught snooping through Steven Eriksen's files!

Chapter

Nine

MS. KRASNER!" George's urgent voice came from the hallway. "Please! I don't need to see—"

"It won't take more than a second," the receptionist interrupted.

Nancy's breath caught in her throat as the office door started to swing inward. She dropped down noiselessly behind the desk, her heart pounding a mile a minute.

"*Oo-ouch!*" George let out an anguished cry. "My ankle—I think I've twisted it!"

George was one of the most coordinated people Nancy knew, so she realized George was just pretending. Peeking under the desk, Nancy saw the door stop halfway open. Yes! The ploy was working!

"Here, let me help you. How bad is it?" the

young woman asked in a voice filled with concern.

"I—I'm not sure. If you could help me back to the other room . . ." Nancy grinned to herself, imagining George's helpless expression.

Nancy quickly returned the file to its drawer and used her bobby pin to lock it again. Then she tiptoed to the door and listened. When she heard the two voices fade, she guessed they were inside the first room. She peeked down the hallway to make sure it was deserted, then ran to the reception area and hurried outside.

She didn't want Eriksen's employee to see her, so she decided to wait for George at a pizzeria across the street. Sure enough, when George came out of the building a few minutes later, the young woman was with her. George was turning her ankle from side to side, trying to convince the receptionist that her ankle was strong enough for her to drive. Finally they said goodbye, and Nancy jogged back across the street to the convertible.

"How's your ankle?" she asked, smiling at George as she hopped into the passenger seat.

George turned in the driver's seat to grin at her. "I seem to have made an amazing recovery. It doesn't hurt at all now." Then, more seriously, she asked, "Did you find anything?"

"Sort of," Nancy answered. "Remember what Richard told us about AeroTech supplying substandard computer equipment to a California military base? Well, Steven Eriksen was implicated in that scandal." She frowned down at the dashboard. "I didn't have time to search the whole office, but I didn't find proof that the same thing is happening at Davis Field *or* that Eriksen had anything to do with Jill's death."

"I guess we'll just have to keep trying," George said optimistically.

Nancy let out a sigh, then checked her watch. "It's only a quarter to five. What time are we supposed to meet Richard for dinner?"

"Not until six-thirty," George told her. "I wouldn't mind doing some shopping before dinner. We passed some clothing stores that looked cool."

"Shopping, huh?" Nancy gave George a sideways glance as she handed over the car keys. Buying clothes wasn't usually a priority for George, but Nancy had a feeling that some of her friend's priorities had shifted since she'd met Richard Mirsky. "Is it serious between you and Richard? Should I start shopping for my bridesmaid's dress?"

"No way! It's not like that with Richard and me," George said, laughing. "Not exactly, anyway." She paused and Nancy said nothing. Finally George continued, "I guess I do like Richard —you know, more than just as a friend. But I'm not sure about getting into a long-distance romance. I've tried it before, and it's really hard."

"Has Richard said anything about how *he* feels?" Nancy asked.

"Actually, he's already talking about visiting me in River Heights," George told her. "I'm not ready to think about that yet."

"Sounds like a good idea," Nancy said. "So for right now, let's concentrate on finding the perfect outfit that will knock Richard's socks off!"

"How do I look, Nancy?" George asked an hour and a half later. She paused on the sidewalk outside Maxine's Garden, the restaurant where they were supposed to meet Richard Mirsky.

"Fantastic," Nancy said. They had found the perfect outfit—a sand-washed silk skirt and matching blouse, both in a soft, rosy red that brought out George's coloring best. The outfit was simple and elegant and suited George's down-to-earth style perfectly.

"I must be crazy," George said with a shaky smile. "I just spent half the money I brought with me to impress a guy I'll probably never see after we leave Florida."

"You don't know that for sure," Nancy argued. "Besides, you might as well make the most of the time you *do* have together."

"I guess." George took a deep breath, then pulled open the restaurant door and went inside. After giving their names to the hostess, Nancy and George followed the young woman out to a courtyard. Roses and azalea bushes edged the courtyard, and old-fashioned cast-iron gas lamps cast a warm glow over the round tables. Richard was at a table at the edge of the courtyard. When he saw George, his whole face lit up.

"Hi, you two," he said, getting to his feet. Taking George's hand, he gave it a squeeze and said in a low voice, "You look great."

"Thanks," George said with a self-conscious smile. "You haven't been waiting long, have you?" she asked as they sat.

Richard pointed to the half-empty glass of seltzer on the table. "Just long enough to drink that. My research was cut short, so I got here early."

When the waiter came a few minutes later, Nancy and Richard ordered shrimp dishes, and George chose pasta primavera. After the waiter delivered sodas for Nancy and George, Richard sat back and said, "What a fiasco today was. It figures that the simulator would go haywire right when I'm getting a demonstration from Steven."

"What happened? You weren't hurt, were you?" George asked worriedly.

"Not at all. It was kind of funny, really," Richard assured her. "Eriksen spent a half hour talking about how invaluable the simulators are and how AeroTech is developing new ones that are even better.

"Anyway, after telling me how AeroTech's simulators are the greatest thing since sliced bread, Eriksen turns one on to give me the demonstration," Richard continued. "But instead of aviation graphics, animated superhero cartoons came on the screen." He let out a husky laugh. "It was pretty amusing."

"I'll bet Eriksen didn't think so," George put in.

"That's for sure. He tried to hide it, but I could tell he was steamed," Richard said. "He swore it was a fluke."

As Nancy listened to his story, her mood became more and more sober. "Either that, or it's further evidence of AeroTech's bad workmanship."

"I don't know," Richard said, giving Nancy a dubious glance. "Cartoon graphics can't just suddenly appear without being programmed into the computer. I doubt that poor workmanship or faulty parts caused the cartoons. It's a lot more likely that someone decided to play a practical joke."

"Maybe," Nancy said, frowning. "All I know for sure is that one of the simulators blew up in my face this morning, and now this has happened. Next time the results could be a lot more serious." She turned as the waiter set down a plate of spiced shrimp and okra in front of her. "Mmm. This smells great!"

After only two short days, Nancy was amazed to see how well George and Richard got along. It was as if they had known each other for years. After they left the restaurant, George and Richard lingered on the sidewalk outside—it was obvious to Nancy that they weren't ready to say good night yet.

Richard stuck his hands in his pants pockets, then turned to George and asked, "How would you like to drive back to Admiral Lewis's house with a charming, irresistible journalist?"

"Sounds good," George said. Then she caught herself and looked at Nancy. "But I *did* come with Nancy . . ."

"Don't worry about it. I can find my way back," Nancy said right away.

George gave Nancy a grateful smile. "Well, if you're sure . . ."

"Positive. I'll be at the beach with my training class all day tomorrow, but I'll talk to you Monday, okay?"

"Okay," George agreed.

Nancy got into her convertible and drove home. When she walked into her house, Yolanda and Diane were both in the living room, studying their NATOPS manuals.

"Hi, stranger," Yolanda greeted her, looking up from her manual. "I heard that you had an action-packed day. Diane tells me you two had quite an adventure on the simulator this morning."

"Not to mention that the whole base was buzzing about your unplanned dead-engine landing," Diane added. "I'm glad to see that you're okay."

"There was some kind of fuel leak. It was pretty hairy," Nancy admitted, without going into detail. "Where's Mary?" she asked, trying to sound casual.

"Out studying her NATOPS with some other trainees from our class," Yolanda replied. "Mary's a great pilot, but she has to work overtime on the mechanical stuff."

If that was true, then Mary wasn't a likely candidate to sabotage the simulators or Jill's plane. But Nancy still wanted to investigate Mary, and this was an opportunity she couldn't pass up. "Well, I'd better get in some studying myself," she said lightly, heading for the stairs. "See you in the A.M."

Upstairs, Nancy slipped quietly into Mary's room and closed the door behind her. Everything was spotlessly neat, Nancy saw. Flowered pillows were arranged on Mary's bed, and photographs and a cosmetics case were on the dresser. The desktop was cleared of everything except a NATOPS manual.

"What's *that* doing here?" Nancy murmured. If Mary was really studying, she would have brought her manual with her. So where *was* she? And why would she lie about it to her roommates?

Nancy frowned, going over to Mary's desk. She opened the NATOPS manual and flipped through it to see if any pages were missing. "One twenty-six—" She drew in her breath sharply when she turned to the next page. Where pages 127 and 128 should have been, there was nothing but a ragged paper edge. The page with 127 and 128 was missing!

So Mary was the person who had eavesdropped on her and George while they examined Jill's plane. Did that necessarily mean that she had also sabotaged Jill's plane? Nancy still hadn't come up with any evidence or motive to support that theory—just the fact that Mary became very edgy whenever Jill's name was mentioned. But George *had* mentioned that Jill and Mary were from the same town.

Nancy looked at the neat row of books that half-filled a shelf above Mary's desk. Most of the books were navy manuals, but at one end was Mary's high school yearbook. Ventura High School, Nancy read from the binding. She pulled the yearbook from the shelf and opened to the pictures of the graduating seniors.

Jill Parker had been married, Nancy recalled. She searched her mind for the girl's maiden name—something like Hanks or—Banks! That was it.

Nancy turned to the *B*'s—then gasped. Jill's name was there, all right. Her photograph was, too, but it had been cut up, leaving a ragged, gaping hole where the face should have been.

Chapter

Ten

A KNOT TWISTED in the pit of Nancy's stomach as she stared at the shreds of Jill's picture. If this was any indication of Mary's feelings toward Jill, maybe she had actually killed Jill.

Nancy wished she knew more about the girls' relationship. She quickly turned to the next page, where she found Mary's photograph. Her dark hair was longer in the photograph than it was now, and her face had a rounder, softer look. Looking at the caption beneath the photo, Nancy read out loud, "'Pom Pom Squad . . . Lifetime member of the C. J. Parker fan club . . .'"

C. J. Parker? Nancy's eyes went back to the name and stayed there. Parker was Jill's married name. But this caption made it sound as if someone named Parker had been *Mary's* high school boyfriend.

Hmm, thought Nancy. She flipped ahead to the *P*'s. C. J. Parker was a handsome blond boy with a wide smile. His caption said that he "never goes anywhere without his football jacket and Mary C." That clinched it. He and Mary *had* been boyfriend and girlfriend. Since Nancy had met her, Mary hadn't mentioned anyone named C.J., or any boyfriend. Maybe she and C.J. had simply gone their separate ways. Or maybe—

Nancy began flipping through the yearbook, looking at the candid shots and funny captions that were sprinkled throughout. There were several pictures of Mary and C.J. They had obviously been a hot item at Ventura High.

"I can't believe what I'm thinking," Nancy murmured. Was it possible that C.J. had dumped Mary and married Jill? If Mary had been as serious about him as these pictures made it seem, that would explain why she had slashed Jill's yearbook picture.

But would she go as far as killing Jill?

Yolanda had mentioned that Mary was weak on the mechanical side of their training, Nancy recalled. It seemed unlikely that she would have an easy time sabotaging Jill's plane. On the other hand, Mary could have gotten someone else to do her dirty work. Someone like Crash Beauford, for instance. That might explain why a man's watch was found in the wreck.

Nancy frowned, thinking of the near accident Mary had had. If she had killed Jill, was the malfunction of Mary's plane simply a coincidence?

A burst of laughter from downstairs startled Nancy from her thoughts. I can't stay in here forever, she realized. Diane and Yolanda could come upstairs at any time.

After closing the yearbook, she returned it to the shelf and quickly searched the rest of Mary's room, but didn't find anything linking Mary to Jill's death. When she was done, she made sure everything was the way she'd found it, then slipped out quietly and went to her room.

Nancy couldn't stop thinking about Mary and Jill. She had to find out what had happened to make Mary hate Jill so much. She wondered if Mary might even try to rekindle her romance with C.J., now that Jill was dead. Tonight when Mary came home, Nancy planned on having a talk with her.

After taking a shower and changing into her nightshirt, Nancy settled against the pillows of her bed and opened her NATOPS manual. I might as well study while I'm waiting for Mary, she thought.

She began reading the material on how to execute a "touch-and-go," when she would touch down her plane and then take off again immediately without stopping. This was to teach trainees how to maneuver landing and taking off from the limited surface of a navy aircraft carrier. The material was interesting, but it had been a hard day. Nancy couldn't stop yawning, and before long her eyes fluttered closed, and she fell asleep.

When Nancy awoke, bright sunlight was shining in her bedroom window and something hard was pressed against her chin. She pushed with her hand, and a book rolled off her chest, hitting the floor with a thud. Peering down with bleary eyes, she saw her NATOPS manual lying there. All at once, the previous night came flooding back to her.

I must have fallen asleep before Mary came home, she realized. She sat up and stretched, then sniffed. It smelled as if her roommates were cooking pancakes, and the delicious aroma made Nancy's stomach growl. She jumped up and went to the bathroom to wash her face. Then she put on her bathing suit, with jean shorts and a T-shirt over it. When she walked into the kitchen fifteen minutes later, Yolanda and Diane were sitting at the table eating pancakes. Mary wasn't with them.

"Are you celebrating something special or do you eat like this every day?" she asked.

"Just on Sundays," Diane said. She pointed to the stack of pancakes in the middle of the table. "Help yourself."

"We work hard six days a week, but on the seventh, we kick back and relax," Yolanda added. "In other words, Sunday is beach day!"

Nancy got a plate and served herself some pancakes with butter and syrup. "I know that's where I'll be today," she said. "I have to meet the rest of my training class there at eleven o'clock for a barbecue and volleyball."

"Well, you won't be alone. Just about every trainee heads to the beach on the weekend," Diane said. "Yolanda and I are leaving right after breakfast, and Mary's already there."

"Oh?" Nancy said. "Maybe I'll see you there then." Regardless of how busy she was with her own training class, she planned on making time to talk with Mary Chambers. This time, she was going to get some straight answers.

The Davis beach was a wide strip of the finest, most brilliant white sand Nancy had ever seen. At the edge of the beach was a picnic area with tables and barbecue grills. Even at ten o'clock the sand was already crowded with sunbathers, swimmers, and joggers. Nancy spotted at least three different volleyball nets. Judging by the clean-cut looks of most of the people, she guessed that there was a high turnout of people from Davis Field Naval Air Station.

The trainees from her class were setting up a volleyball net just beyond a concessions stand, but Nancy didn't go over to them right away. Shielding her eyes from the sun, she scanned the beach for Mary. She finally spotted her jogging along the water's edge in a sleek red one-piece suit. Nancy broke into a jog herself and ran down to the hard-packed, wet sand to meet Mary.

"Hi. Mind if we talk for a minute?" Nancy asked.

Mary stopped running, breathing hard. "Yeah. Okay," she said. Nancy knew she wasn't crazy about the idea.

"We haven't had much of a chance to get to know each other," Nancy said with a smile. "I mean, even though we're living in the same house and all, we keep missing each other."

She was trying to put Mary at ease, hoping to get her to open up, but Mary just tapped her sneaker on the sand and said, "What do you want to know?"

"I don't know . . . Where you're from, what you're interested in."

Mary's gaze flitted nervously over the beach. "I'm from Ventura, Kentucky, and what I'm interested in is becoming a fighter pilot," she said curtly. "Anything else?"

Nancy ignored her rude tone. "Ventura, Kentucky, huh? Isn't that where Jill Parker was from, too?"

Apparently that was the wrong question to ask. Mary fixed Nancy with an angry, piercing gaze. "Look, my private life is none of your business." With that, Mary took off down the beach again, her sneakers pounding into the sand.

Whoa! Nancy thought. Talk about touchy! She was still staring after Mary, when some guys' voices caught her attention. As she turned toward the group of three who were jogging along the shore, Nancy identified Crash Beauford. As he and the others passed Nancy, Crash lifted his mirrored sunglasses and, saying nothing, simply stared at her.

Keep your distance, Drew, Nancy ordered herself, feeling the heat rise to her cheeks. She nodded curtly, then turned away and ran to join her training class.

For the next several hours Nancy played volleyball, swam, and gorged herself on burgers and potato salad. After the rigorous pace of her case *and* her training the last couple of days, it felt great to allow herself to have fun. Her training class was divided into three squadrons, and the volleyball competition was between squadrons. By the middle of the afternoon, Nancy's squadron, Squadron 1, was playing the final match against Squadron 3. Nancy had just finished serving when a familiar face next to the concessions stand caught her attention.

Steven Eriksen was standing there in striped swim trunks, talking to a short, heavier man wearing a straw hat, sunglasses, and a Hawaiian shirt over his bathing suit. Even from where she was, some twenty yards away, Nancy saw the tense set of Eriksen's face. While she watched, the two men stepped away from the stand and into the empty area around the side, where the stand was butted up against a dune.

What's going on? she wondered, her suspicions immediately aroused.

"Heads up!" a voice broke into her thoughts.

Nancy blinked as the volleyball dropped to the

sand right in front of her. "Sorry," she apologized to her teammates. "I think I need to take a break."

What she really wanted to do was get closer to Steven Eriksen and the other man so she could find out what they were talking about.

Nancy had only taken a few steps toward the concessions stand when Rhonda Kisch's voice sounded right behind her. "What's the matter, Ensign? Is the competition too much for you?"

Nancy turned to her On Wing and automatically saluted. "No, sir!"

Rhonda Kisch and another woman were standing there. They were both wearing bathing suits and hats, but even civilian clothing didn't soften Rhonda's stern appearance. "Maybe you think it's just a game, but when I see a pilot who deserts her teammates at a critical moment, I have to ask myself: How will she react when her fellow pilots are depending on her in the air, under fire?"

"Sir! I've been playing for hours and I, uh, need something to drink." Nancy stifled a groan. Once again, she couldn't explain her actions without breaking her cover. Why was it that Rhonda Kisch always saw her in the worst possible light?

Rhonda Kisch raised a dubious eyebrow. "Well, after a day of rest I would like to intensify our training a little. I'll expect you for FAM-Two tomorrow morning at oh-six hundred hours."

Nancy gaped at her On Wing. That was six in

the morning! Somehow she forced herself to salute and say, "Yes, sir."

"See you then, Ensign." With that Lieutenant Kisch and the other woman continued down the beach.

Great, Nancy thought, rolling her eyes. But she didn't have time to stand around complaining about her flight training. She looked back at the concessions stand, then groaned. Neither Steven Eriksen nor the other man was there anymore!

They've got to be around here somewhere, Nancy thought, and just then spotted the other man's Hawaiian shirt. He was heading toward the parking lot. As Nancy followed the man, her thoughts flashed on Rhonda Kisch. Was it just a coincidence that the On Wing had stopped her at that exact moment? Or had the lieutenant been trying to distract her?

Up ahead, the man in the Hawaiian shirt got into a green sedan, so Nancy hurried to her car and slipped behind the wheel. She started her engine, then waited, keeping an eye on the sedan. After a few moments the car headed for the exit.

Nancy was just putting her own car into gear when she heard a scuffling noise on the pavement outside her door. A split second later something sharp and heavy struck the back of her head.

"Ow!" Nancy felt a sharp stab of pain. Then everything went black.

Chapter

Eleven

NANCY WAS DIMLY AWARE of a light somewhere nearby and of a painful throbbing at the back of her head. Slowly, she opened her eyes and found herself staring at the red dashboard of her convertible. She was lying on her side across the front seat. Late afternoon sunlight washed over her, and she could hear the sounds of waves breaking.

"Oooh," she moaned. Her hand moved to the back of her head. She winced when it touched the swollen knot there. That's right, she recalled groggily. Someone had knocked her out in the parking lot at the Davis beach. Something wasn't right, she realized. She no longer heard the shouts and cries of beach-goers. It was so peaceful and quiet—the only sounds were the squawking of sea gulls and the lap of gently rolling waves.

Carefully she tried to push herself up to a sitting position. "This isn't Davis beach," she murmured out loud. She was parked at the side of a small road next to a deserted beach. White dunes rose on one side of the road and a vast, empty stretch of sand and sea grass were behind a fence on the other side.

Whoever knocked me out must have driven me here and left me, Nancy realized. The person probably didn't want anyone at the crowded beach to know I'd been attacked. Checking her watch, Nancy saw that it was almost six-thirty. She'd been out for at least half an hour.

Trying to ignore the pain in the back of her head, she got out of her car and looked around. On the fence that ran next to the road was a sign that read State Park—Keep Out. Apparently, people took the warning seriously because there wasn't a single other person or car in sight.

Nancy frowned, replaying in her head all that had happened just before she was knocked out. She was about to follow the man she'd seen talking to Steven Eriksen. Could Eriksen have seen her heading after him and decided to stop her? The man in the Hawaiian shirt hadn't the trim, clean-cut looks of most navy personnel, but maybe he was Eriksen's man on the inside. Maybe it was *his* watch she'd found in Jill's plane, and not Crash's. Or maybe Crash had knocked her out to keep her from getting too close to Eriksen and the other man.

After the cool treatment Mary had given her,

Nancy had to consider her a suspect, too. Nancy wasn't sure what Mary might have to do with Steven Eriksen, but she couldn't rule out any suspects yet. One thing was clear: whoever had knocked her out didn't want her to follow the man with the Hawaiian shirt.

"I just wish I knew who he was," she said in a frustrated rush. "I'm not going to be able to find out by sitting here, though."

Gingerly rubbing the back of her head, Nancy returned to the car and got behind the wheel, then turned the key in the ignition.

Nothing.

When she looked at the fuel indicator, she saw that the needle was pointing at the *E*. "Great," she muttered, hitting the steering wheel in frustration. "I'm out of gas and probably miles from the nearest gas station!"

The person who'd knocked her out must have siphoned out the gas in her tank. Nancy peered up and down the deserted beach road. "I guess I'd better start walking. . . ."

When Nancy walked in the front door of her house, Yolanda was standing in the foyer, wearing a sleeveless knit dress and sandals. She had been using the mirror over the small table there to apply her lipstick. When she saw Nancy, she straightened up.

"Nancy, where've you been? Some guy from your squadron named Stu left a message. He wondered if you were all right because you disappeared so abruptly from the volleyball tournament."

"It's a long story," Nancy said truthfully. "In a nutshell, I ran out of gas and it took me this long to get back." She didn't want her housemates to worry or get suspicious about her, so she didn't say anything more. "Do you have a date?" she asked, changing the subject.

"Sort of. A guy from my squadron is picking me up, and we're going out for dessert and coffee," Yolanda answered.

"Where's everyone else?" Nancy asked. It was really only Mary that Nancy was interested in talking to, but she didn't want Yolanda to know that.

"Diane's still at the beach at a barbecue," Yolanda told her. "Mary's upstairs. She said something about being wiped out and went to sleep. She asked not to be disturbed."

Hmm, thought Nancy. Maybe the reason Mary was so tired was that she'd used up a lot of energy knocking out Nancy and leaving her stranded in the middle of nowhere. "Was Mary at the beach all day? Did she ever leave?" Nancy asked.

Yolanda shrugged. "I guess she was there all day." A horn sounded in front of the house, and she headed for the door. "There's my date. See you later."

"'Bye." Nancy went into the living room and flopped down on the couch, totally exhausted. In the couple of days since she'd arrived at Davis Field, she'd been knocked out, her plane had been sabotaged, and she'd had a computer screen blow up in her face. She had to be getting close to finding out who had sabotaged Jill's plane—close enough to make someone very nervous.

Then why did she feel as if she were still at square one?

The next morning Nancy's alarm woke her before five. Ugh, she thought. Her head still hurt, and she felt as if someone had stuffed her skull with cotton.

I'd give anything to be able to relax today, she thought, but knew that rest wouldn't be on Lieutenant Kisch's schedule for the morning.

Nancy got up and dressed in her work uniform, then tiptoed downstairs and outside to her car. When she drove up to the hangar at the south airfield, it was a quarter to six. There wasn't much activity at the base. Nancy had passed only one or two other cars, and the south airfield was completely deserted and quiet.

She didn't even realize that she'd started to doze off until the sound of an approaching car jolted her awake again. As Rhonda Kisch drove up in her blue sedan, Nancy got out of her convertible and saluted. At least I'm not late today, she thought.

Lieutenant Kisch got out of her car and returned Nancy's salute. Then she said crisply, "Let's get to work, Ensign."

For the first hour of their session, Nancy and her On Wing reviewed the technique for doing touch-and-gos. Despite her weariness and the dull throbbing at the back of her head, Nancy was able to answer all of the lieutenant's questions correctly.

Finally Lieutenant Kisch turned to her and said, "Let's see if you can fly as well as you can talk, Ensign. I've assigned you a new Mentor. Let's take her up, and you can try a few touch-and-gos on the landing strip."

As soon as Nancy strapped into her new T-34C, her weariness evaporated and she felt the incredible thrill of handling a powerful plane. With her On Wing giving her instructions from the rear position, Nancy took off several minutes later. The airspace and Mentor both seemed familiar now. Rhonda Kisch directed Nancy through a shortened route over the Gulf of Mexico, then ordered her to fly back to the airstrip to execute her first touch-and-go.

Adrenaline pumped through Nancy as she approached the airfield, dropped her power to 150 knots, and went through her landing checklist: "Landing gear out—parking breaks off—breaks pumped firm—landing lights on . . ." she murmured into her microphone.

Below her, the landing field was fast approaching. "Rolling out on the downwind," she said. Nancy dropped the Mentor closer to the landing field and banked around so that she was flying downwind. This was the last step before pulling the plane in a complete turnaround so that she would be flying *into* the wind when she landed.

Seconds later Nancy made the 180-degree turn and brought the Mentor down toward the landing strip. "Power down," she said. She cut the engine and angled the plane to a smooth landing. As soon as she felt the wheels touch down, she hit the throttle and pushed the Mentor back to takeoff speed. "Power to the max. I'm up again."

Immediately the plane was airborne and she was shooting toward the Gulf of Mexico once again. Nancy could barely keep herself from letting out a hoot of victory. She had done it!

When Nancy brought the Mentor down for a final landing two hours later, her spirits were high. During the debriefing session that followed, her On Wing evaluated Nancy's performance. She didn't give any praise, but Nancy noticed that she didn't have much criticism, either.

When the debriefing was over, Nancy headed for the wall of lockers along the side wall of the hangar. Her stomach growled, reminding her that she hadn't eaten since the night before. Maybe she'd call George at Admiral Lewis's office to see if she wanted to take a break and join her for a late breakfast. She twirled the combination to her lock, then popped it open. Nancy tried to remember if George had plans with Richard Mirsky for that day—

Ka-booom!

As Nancy pulled open on her locker, an explosion ripped the door from its hinges!

Chapter

Twelve

NANCY WAS CATAPULTED backward with amazing force. She threw her arms in front of her face, and a second later her hip hit the cement floor. Metal debris showered over her as she curled her body into a ball to protect herself. Her heart was pounding, and she felt as if her entire body were in shock. After a few moments she heard footsteps clicking rapidly toward her.

"Ensign Drew! Are you all right?"

Slowly Nancy lifted her head to see Lieutenant Kisch crouched next to her. Several more people were running toward them from other parts of the hangar.

"I th-think so," Nancy said. She touched her hip, but it didn't seem to be injured. When she turned to look at her On Wing, she saw that Rhonda was gaping at the row of lockers. Nancy followed the lieutenant's gaze—and her mouth fell open.

"Whoa!" was all she could say.

Her locker had been completely blown away— the spot where it had been was now nothing but a yawning hole. The door was lying in a twisted heap a few feet from Nancy.

"The show's over, folks. Ensign Drew is all right, so you can go back to what you were doing." Lieutenant Kisch waved away the knot of people who had gathered around Nancy. When she and Nancy were alone, the lieutenant lowered her voice and asked, "What happened, Ensign?"

Frowning, Nancy stood up and walked over to her locker space. After checking the debris for a few moments, she found what she suspected. "Plastic explosives," she said, pointing to a yellow puttylike substance that was splattered around the shell of the locker. "Someone set it so it would go off when I opened my locker door."

The lieutenant turned to Nancy with a frown. "First a cut fuel line, and now this. What's going on here?"

Nancy decided to take a chance and level with her On Wing. After all, the saboteur had put Rhonda Kisch's life in danger, too. And none of the clues pointed to Rhonda's involvement. Taking a deep breath, Nancy told the lieutenant her real reason for being at the naval air station. "Obviously, someone doesn't want me to find out who sabotaged Jill's plane," she finished.

"That's why I've been the target of attacks. I'm sorry I didn't tell you sooner, sir, but I'm under strict orders from Admiral Lewis not to talk about the case with *anyone.*"

The On Wing listened to Nancy's explanation without saying a word, but her face expressed more and more concern. "You'll understand if I check this out with the admiral?" she said when Nancy was done.

Nancy stifled a sigh. "Yes, sir," she said. It figured that Rhonda Kisch wouldn't take anything she said at face value. Then again, maybe that was one of the things that made her a good officer.

Lieutenant Kisch excused Nancy with a salute, then hurried from the hangar. Nancy assumed she was going straight to Admiral Lewis's office. Nancy had to contact the admiral too, to see if he knew anything about the man with the Hawaiian shirt she'd seen with Steven Eriksen the day before. But first, she had to do some investigating right here.

Nancy's gaze swept over the hangar, taking in the faces of the dozen or so trainees and flight instructors who were in and around the planes. She didn't see Crash or Mary anywhere. Her next step was to check the logbook. She jogged over to the table next to the hangar's huge rolling door, where the book was kept. Nancy had placed her manual and shoulder bag in her locker at the start of her training session. She hadn't seen any sign of explosives then, which meant that the person who'd planted the plastic explosive had done it while she was in the air. She skimmed the list of people who'd signed in that morning.

"Steven Eriksen!" she murmured, reading the name from the logbook. He'd signed in at seven o'clock that morning, listing as his purpose "to inspect computer controls." He had signed out at nine-thirty, about a half hour before she finished her flight training session.

Nancy tapped the page with her forefinger. According to the logbook, only two other trainees and their On Wings had been in the hangar when Eriksen had arrived. It couldn't hurt to question them. Neither trainee had signed out yet, but when Nancy tried to track them down, she learned they were both still in the air.

Nancy was debating what to do, when her stomach rumbled again. I'll drive home to change and get something to eat, she thought. Her bag and everything in it had been ruined in the blast, but luckily she'd left her car keys under the sun visor in the convertible.

Nancy drove to the exit, where the security guard waved her through. She pulled up behind a red convertible sports car waiting for the light to change. She gave an idle glance at the dark-haired young man behind the wheel—then did a double take.

It was Crash Beauford! The light turned green, and Crash turned left, heading in the direction of the town of Davis. Nancy pulled left behind

Crash. Since I'm going that way anyway, she thought, I might as well see what Crash Beauford is up to. She slowed a little to put some distance between them. She was glad she'd put up the top to protect the seats from the hot sun—if she was lucky, Crash wouldn't recognize her or her car.

After a few minutes he turned off the local highway onto Main Street, which ran through the center of Davis. Nancy followed him past a row of stores, then when he parked in front of the town's post office.

Nancy pulled her car into a spot across the street. She didn't want to appear too obvious, so she shifted her rearview mirror so that she could keep an eye on Crash without turning to stare at him. Crash got out of his car and jogged inside the post office.

Wait a minute, Nancy thought. Davis Field has its *own* post office, and Crash had just been at the base. Why come all the way here?

Nancy was turning the question over in her mind, when something else caught her eye. A man had just come out of the post office and was getting into a green sedan. Nancy immediately recognized his straw hat and rotund build. It was the same man she'd seen talking to Steven Eriksen at the beach right before she was knocked out! Maybe it was just a coincidence that he and Crash were at the same place at the same time. On the other hand . . .

Nancy put her car into gear as the green sedan

pulled into the road. "This time I'm going to find out where you're—"

Just then a big truck pulled in front of Nancy, blocking her view. She leaned on her horn and waved, but the driver merely shrugged and gestured for her to pull around him. By the time Nancy backed up and angled around the truck, she didn't see the green sedan anywhere. She sped to the next intersection but the sedan was nowhere in sight. "I don't believe this," she muttered. Stifling a sigh, Nancy turned around and drove back to the post office. When she reached the low brick building, Crash's car was gone, so she pulled into the spot he had just vacated.

Even if I can't follow that man, she thought, maybe I can find out what he was doing here.

She went inside the post office and found herself in a small service area. Zip code books, forms, and envelopes sat on a table next to the door, and a row of mailboxes ran along the wall to the right. Across from the door was a counter with a middle-aged woman in a postal uniform behind it. "Can I help you?" she asked.

Nancy flashed the woman a bright smile. "My boyfriend was just here. A dark-haired guy with sunglasses," she said, making up the story as she went along. "He thinks he might have dropped his wallet."

"A wallet?" The woman shot a glance at the wall of old-fashioned metal mailboxes. "He was just over there getting his mail. Second box from the left, top row. I don't see anything on the floor near there."

Nancy hurried over to the box. While she pretended to search the floor area, she glanced at the box. The top half was glass, and Nancy could see that it was empty. "You didn't notice if anyone else was over there, did you? Maybe someone took it by mistake?"

"There was only one other customer around while your friend was here, and he left a letter for Mr. Beauford, as a matter of fact. Isn't that your friend's name, Eddie Beauford?"

"Yes," Nancy said, trying not to show her excitement. "Well, I guess my boyfriend must have dropped his wallet somewhere else. Thanks, anyway."

Her mind was spinning as she left the post office. So the man with the visor *did* know Crash. How did Steven Eriksen know him? Were all three connected?

Maybe a shower will help me to see things more clearly, she thought. Ten minutes later she pulled to a stop in front of her house. As she got out of the car, she heard the shrill ringing of the phone inside. Nancy ran up the steps, unlocked the door, and raced for the kitchen, grabbing the extension there.

"Hello?" she said breathlessly.

"Nancy! Boy, am I glad you're there!"

It was George, and judging by the tone of her

voice, she was calling about something important. "What's up?" Nancy asked, gripping the receiver more tightly.

"You've got to come to Admiral Lewis's office right away!" George said urgently. "I think I've trapped Jill's murderer!"

Chapter

Thirteen

"WHAT!" NANCY WAS SO SURPRISED that she almost dropped the receiver.

"I don't have time to explain," George's urgent whisper came over the line. "Just get over to the admiral's office right away!"

"I'm on my way." Nancy slammed down the receiver and ran back to her car. After finally pulling up in front of the administration bloc, she parked and raced inside and up the stairs.

George was waiting in the hallway next to the admiral's outer office, her arms crossed over her chest and her eyes fixed on something down the hall. When she saw Nancy, she hurried over to her and said in a low voice, "Boy, am I glad you're here."

"Who did you trap? Where is the person? What happened, George?" The questions came rolling off Nancy's tongue so quickly that George had to hold up a hand to stop her.

"Okay, here's the story," she said in a whisper. "I was going to return the personnel files to the classified files room, where Admiral Lewis keeps them. Fran usually keeps it locked, but when I went to use the key, the door was already unlocked. Fran called in sick today, so I knew she didn't unlock it, and the admiral's in a meeting."

"So who was it?" Nancy asked.

"I still don't know. I pushed open the door, but there aren't any windows inside. The room was totally dark except for a flashlight beam at the far end of the room. I figured that anyone who was in there for legitimate reasons would turn on the light. I wasn't sure what to do, so I called you right away."

While she spoke, George led Nancy down the hall beyond the admiral's office, to a door marked Classified. "I've been keeping an eye on the door ever since," George added. "Whoever's in there hasn't left."

"Then I think it's time we found out who it is and what they're up to," Nancy whispered. She put a finger to her lips, then silently turned the doorknob and pushed the door open.

As George had said, the room was dark except for the glow from a flashlight near the rear wall. The beam gave enough light for Nancy to see four rows of tall filing cabinets. The person with the flashlight was in the farthest row from the doorway. Nancy couldn't see who it was, but it sounded as if he or she were going through some files.

Nancy signaled George to stay by the door in case the person tried to make a run for it. Then she closed the door quietly behind them so as not to draw attention from the hallway light. Her pulse was racing as she tiptoed past the rows of files. She hardly dared to breathe for fear that whoever was there would hear. Moving slowly and silently, she made her way to the last row of files and stuck her head around the corner.

Nancy immediately recognized Mary Chambers halfway down the row of cabinets, bent over an open drawer. Mary held her flashlight with one hand while she flipped through the papers of one of the files with the other.

"I think you'll be able to see better with the lights on, Mary," Nancy spoke up.

Mary straightened up and dropped the file and flashlight. A second later George hit the switch and the room flooded with fluorescent light. Mary took a few steps toward the door, but then stopped when she saw George circling around to her from the other side of the room.

"What do you want with me?" she finally asked, her eyes flitting nervously between Nancy and George.

Nancy decided to be direct. "What are you doing, Mary?" Nancy asked.

"I don't have to tell you anything," Mary said angrily.

"Then, why don't I tell *you* a few things,"

Nancy said. "I know you were spying on George and me when we examined Jill's plane—you dropped a page from your NATOPS manual there."

"Did you kill Jill?" George asked, stepping forward. "Is that why you've been acting so strangely around Nancy, because you don't want her to learn that Jill's death wasn't an accident?"

"You two don't know what you're talking about. Why would I kill Jill?" Mary said without hesitating, but Nancy noticed the uncertain glimmer in her eyes. "Look, I don't have to sit around here and let you two give me the third degree."

She pushed past George and started toward the door, then stopped short with another gasp. "Admiral Lewis!" She jolted to attention and gave a salute.

Looking over, Nancy saw that the admiral's powerful frame filled the doorway. "Ensign Drew is here at my request," he told Mary. "I *strongly* suggest that you cooperate with her, Ensign . . ."

"Ensign Chambers, sir," Mary supplied.

The admiral told her she could be at ease. "I think it's about time we got to the bottom of this situation," he added. "I want all three of you in my office, pronto."

The three girls followed Admiral Lewis to his inner office and sat in a row in front of his desk. Nancy and George filled him in on how they'd found Mary in the classified files room and on Nancy's guess that Mary was bitter because her high school boyfriend had married Jill Parker. As they spoke, Nancy noticed that Mary's face was turning redder and redder.

"What do you have to say for yourself, Ensign Chambers?" the admiral asked when Nancy and George were finished.

"It's not like it sounds," Mary said in a small voice. "I didn't kill Jill, I swear!"

George rolled her eyes, but Admiral Lewis simply folded his hands on his desk and said, "Go on."

Mary took a deep breath, then said, "Look, maybe I used to hate Jill, but that was a long time ago. When C.J. told me he was dumping me to marry her, I admit that I went a little ballistic. I did stuff like slashing her picture. I even used to call her house and make threats." Nancy could tell that it still hurt her to think about what had happened.

"It was the worst time of my whole life, but at least something good came out of it," Mary went on. "My guidance counselor at high school was pretty cool. We kept in touch even after I went to college. Anyway, she's the one who first suggested that I join the navy. She said it had really helped her brother to get his act together. I did it as a last resort, but now I'm really glad." She gave the admiral a shaky smile. "Being in the navy made me realize that I have a lot going for me, even though I'm not with C.J. anymore."

"How did Jill end up in the navy?" George

asked. "I mean, isn't it amazing that both of you ended up in the fighter pilot training program at the same time?"

"I'll say," Mary said, shaking her head. "Jill and I talked about that. It turns out that her older brother is a fighter pilot. He loves it so much that Jill decided she wanted in on the action, too. She was going through her training here while C.J. went to grad school back in Kentucky."

"So you're saying that you didn't hate Jill?" Nancy asked.

"Not a bit," Mary answered, shaking her head adamantly. "I admit I was shocked when I first saw her here. But pretty soon I realized that my life is a lot fuller now than when I was with C.J. I was amazed to realize that I didn't even mind that he and Jill were married. I mean, Jill and I decided to be housemates. I never would have done that if I still hated her."

Mary seemed sincere, but Nancy still had a lot of unanswered questions. "If you didn't sabotage Jill's plane, then why were you snooping around the hangar where her plane is being stored?" George asked. "And what were you doing just now in the admiral's classified files?"

Mary took a deep breath and let it out slowly. "I've been trying to find out who killed Jill," she said earnestly. "I was waiting until I came up with concrete proof before I said anything. I knew that if anyone found out about the bad blood between me and Jill, I'd be a suspect."

"What made you think Jill was murdered?" Admiral Lewis asked Mary. "The report stated that her death was accidental."

"Well, whoever made the report must not know that Jill was looking into some illegal activity here at Davis Field," Mary said hotly. "She didn't tell me exactly what it was, but she hinted that when the news broke, it was going to create a huge scandal."

Nancy caught the meaningful look George gave her. Maybe Jill *had* been looking into AeroTech. If she broke the story that the company had knowingly provided the navy with defective equipment, that would certainly qualify as a "huge scandal." "Have you found out what Jill was investigating?" Nancy asked Mary.

"I think it has something to do with the computer simulators." Mary pressed her lips together, frowning. "After the . . . accident, I found some stuff in Jill's room." Mary opened her shoulder bag and pulled out a handwritten list, which she handed to Admiral Lewis.

"Hmm. It looks like Jill was keeping track of malfunctions on the computer simulators," he murmured, skimming the list. "'Failure to boot up' . . . 'Graphics not responding properly to controls.'" He read a few more items from the list. "The incidents go back to a few weeks before her plane crashed. And look—"

Admiral Lewis frowned and handed the sheet to Nancy, pointing about halfway down the list.

Next to the entry, Jill had written the word *Sabotage* in red pencil, followed by a question mark.

"Whoa!" George exclaimed, reading over Nancy's shoulder. "So she definitely suspected foul play."

"I found something else, too," Mary said excitedly. She reached into her bag again and retrieved a stiff sheet from inside her NATOPS manual. Leaning forward, Nancy saw that it was a diagram of the T-34C. The diagram had been photocopied onto two pages, which had been placed back to back, then laminated between two sheets of plastic. The name *Beauford* had been printed in felt-tip pen at the upper left corner, but otherwise the diagram looked identical to the one in Nancy's NATOPS manual.

"Why would Jill have Crash's diagram of the Mentor?" Nancy wondered aloud. She took the laminated sheet and turned it over in her hands. "She would have had the same diagram in her own NATOPS manual."

"Maybe Crash was the person sabotaging the simulators," George suggested. "Didn't you say you found a sheet of blue paper next to the simulator that exploded, just like the piece of paper you saw in the NATOPS manual at his house?" When Nancy nodded, George pointed to the diagram and said, "Jill may have thought this was evidence."

"Evidence of what, though?" Nancy asked,

shaking her head. "Jill got this diagram *before* her plane crashed."

"I don't understand why Jill would consider this important," the admiral put in, staring at the laminated sheet. "Fighter pilot trainees have to memorize that diagram just to get past FAM-0. Crash is at a much more advanced stage of his training, *and* he's a top pilot. He wouldn't need to refer to that in order to sabotage a T-Thirty-four C."

Mary's eyes flashed. "But I just *know* he's up to no good! Otherwise Jill wouldn't have kept his diagram!" she burst out.

"I feel the same way," Nancy said, fingering the edge of the laminated diagram. "But so far I don't see what . . ." She let her voice trail off, then peered at the plastic more carefully. "Hey! There's a slit in the side of the plastic, where the two sides aren't stuck together."

The opening was just big enough for her to probe between the two photocopied sheets with her forefinger. "Something's in here!" she exclaimed, and pulled out a small square of folded-up newspaper. The article that had been clipped was a few years old. "'Honors Student Caught in Grade-Changing Scandal,'" she read the headline. After glancing at the first few lines, she looked at the others in shock. "You guys, this is about Crash. Apparently, he was involved in a computerized grade-changing scam at his college."

"Cheating?" Admiral Lewis frowned darkly. "The navy never would have accepted him into the fighter pilot training program with that on his record."

"Maybe he found a way to cover it up," George said, shrugging. "Didn't you say he has a lot of navy brass in his family? Maybe one of them convinced the right people to overlook that part of his record."

"I *knew* Crash was a weasel," Mary said. "But what does his college record have to do with what's been going on here?"

Nancy's gaze had fallen on a note at the bottom of the article that was written in a very familiar back-slanted handwriting: "Follow orders, or a copy of this goes to Admiral Lewis." She let out a whistle, holding out the article so that the others could see the note. "Someone is blackmailing Crash," she said. "The same person who wrote the notes on that blue paper."

"I can't believe I've had that article this whole time, and didn't even know it!" Mary said. She gave Nancy a sheepish look and added, "I owe you an apology, by the way."

Nancy had a feeling she knew what Mary was about to say. "You locked me into Crash's closet, didn't you?" she guessed.

Mary nodded. "I had just sneaked into his house myself when you got there. I hid behind the door to his room, but I knew you'd find me there eventually, so I locked you in the closet and bolted. I knew Crash was due home soon so you wouldn't be stuck for too long." She took a deep breath and added, "I also wrote that note warning you off the case. It's been my personal mission to find Jill's killer. Maybe it's my way of trying to make up for all the terrible stuff I did when she and C.J. first got together."

"Did you happen to get a look at the note sticking out of Crash's NATOPS manual?" Nancy asked. "It was on blue paper, and it had this same handwriting on it."

Mary shook her head.

"Well, you've answered *some* of the questions that have been nagging me," Nancy said slowly. "But I still don't see how AeroTech fits in. I mean, until now, the theory that makes the most sense is that AeroTech got Crash to sabotage Jill's plane so that she couldn't expose the fact that they were providing the navy with inferior computer equipment."

"But Jill suspected that someone—maybe Crash—was sabotaging the simulators. Why would AeroTech sabotage their own equipment? That would just make their problems worse," Mary said.

"We've been wondering about that, too," Nancy said, frowning. "Still, Steven Eriksen *has* been acting weird." Turning to Admiral Lewis, she told him about the short, heavyset man she'd seen with Eriksen at the beach. "The same man left something for Crash at the post office in town this morning," she finished. "My instincts tell me that he's involved in the case, but I'm not sure how. Is there any chance he works here at the base?"

The admiral shook his head. "On any given day, there are over twenty thousand people at Davis Field," he said. "I can't keep track of them all. Still, I think it's time to take action."

"W-what are you going to do?" Mary asked nervously.

"I'm going to call Crash Beauford in for questioning. I've got an important meeting now, but I want him waiting for me here when I get back. Once I talk to him, I'm sure he'll see that it's in his best interests to tell us exactly what he's been doing and who he's been doing it for."

Admiral Lewis got to his feet and turned to Mary. "Ensign Chambers, I'll decide what measures to take with you after I speak with Ensign Beauford."

"Yes, sir," Mary said quietly. "Sir, are we through? I'm due at the south airfield."

"You're dismissed," the admiral told her. "Nancy, George, I'd like you to meet me back here at five this afternoon so you can be on hand while I speak with Beauford."

Nancy and George promised to be there, then left. Lingering outside the building, George asked, "So where do we go from here?"

Nancy frowned. Despite all that they had learned, she felt edgy. "I'm not sure why, but I feel as if we're overlooking something important," she said, half to herself.

George didn't seem to be listening. Her eyes

focused on something behind Nancy, and a big smile spread across her face. "Richard! Hi!" she called.

Nancy turned to see Richard Mirsky walking toward them, holding a notebook with several papers sticking out of it. "Hi, yourself," he told George, giving her a quick kiss on the cheek. "Hi, Nancy."

As he turned to her, he shifted the notebook in his hand, and a few of the sheets fell to the pavement. He and Nancy both bent to pick them up. Most of the sheets were typewritten, but Nancy froze when she saw the notes that were penciled in on the margins.

"George, look at that writing!" she said.

George followed her gaze, then drew in her breath sharply. "It's back-slanted—exactly the same as the writing of whoever's blackmailing Crash!"

"What are you two talking about?" Richard asked, perplexed. "This doesn't have anything to do with your case. It's just some information I got at a meeting I had with the technical director from Howard Technologies—a guy named Olmstead."

George blinked. "Olmstead? Isn't he the man Admiral Lewis met with on Saturday? Remember, Nan? You saw him, too."

"That's right! Why didn't I think of it before?" Nancy felt a light blink on inside her head. "AeroTech isn't blackmailing Crash—Howard Technologies is!"

Chapter
Fourteen

W HAT!" GEORGE AND RICHARD EXCLAIMED at the same time.

Nancy let out her breath in a rush. "Now I know why the man I saw at the beach looked familiar," she said, thinking out loud.

"Of course! Olmstead is short and kind of heavy," George put in. "It had to be him!"

"In his beach clothes, he looked different from when we saw him here," Nancy went on. "And his visor partially hid his face. I didn't make the connection until right now, but it makes sense. Olmstead is trying to take the navy contract for simulators and computer components away from AeroTech."

"And you think he's doing that by making sure that AeroTech looks bad?" Richard asked, still slightly confused.

"By blackmailing *Crash* into making sure AeroTech looks bad," Nancy corrected. "I bet anything that's the scandal Jill was checking out. She must have figured out what was going on, and Crash and Howard Technologies decided to kill her before she could expose them."

"But didn't you say Olmstead was talking to Steven Eriksen when you saw him at the beach?" George asked. "Why would they be talking to each other when they're competitors?"

"Eriksen seemed pretty steamed," Nancy recalled, thinking back. "Maybe he was starting to get suspicious about all the 'accidents' that were making AeroTech look so bad. Maybe that's why he set up a meeting with Olmstead, to confront him."

"So, it's Crash and Olmstead," Richard said, rubbing his beard thoughtfully. "I guess it makes sense. Olmstead wouldn't have free access to the planes or the simulators, so he needed someone inside the base to do his dirty work for him."

"He dug up that article on the grade-changing scheme and used it to blackmail Crash," Nancy added. "He and Crash wouldn't want to be seen together, which was why Crash got that post office box in town. That way, Bob Olmstead could leave him instructions without their having any direct contact.

"He must have decided to get me out of the way, once he heard that I was sneaking around Crash's house," Nancy went on. "So Crash cut my fuel line. He probably expected that I'd have an 'accident,' the way Jill did, and that the impact and fire would hide any evidence of foul play."

"I wonder if Crash had a sense that Mary was onto him and Olmstead, too? By sabotaging the computer controls of her plane, they could get her out of the way *and* make AeroTech look bad at the same time," George said, shaking her head in disgust. "Talk about depraved. Olmstead obviously doesn't care who he hurts, as long as his company gets the contract."

"Olmstead will probably get a hefty bonus from Howard Technologies if he lands the contract," Richard put in. "It's unbelievable how low some people will sink because of greed."

"Olmstead's not the only criminal," Nancy pointed out. "Even if he was being blackmailed, Crash is as much a murderer as Bob Olmstead."

"You guys—" George looked back and forth between Nancy and Richard, biting her lip. "This guy is dangerous. Shouldn't we tell Admiral Lewis?"

"He's in a meeting until five, remember? But I don't think we can afford to wait that long," Nancy said worriedly. "Who knows *what* Olmstead is up to right now."

For a moment the three of them stood there staring at one another. Then Richard snapped his fingers and said, "I just thought of a way we might be able to prove Bob Olmstead's guilt! He's staying in a motel near the beach." He glanced briefly at his notebook. "The Pink Flamingo. I have the address and phone number right here."

When Nancy, George, and Richard pulled into the parking lot of the Pink Flamingo, Nancy didn't see Bob Olmstead's green sedan anywhere. They inquired at the office and found out that Olmstead's room was on the second floor. Nancy rapped twice on the door, just to be safe. When no one answered, she took a credit card from her wallet and used it to pop the lock. Then, she, Richard, and George hurried inside the room.

The room was modern, with two beds and a built-in Formica desk between them. There was a shiny chrome rack for clothes, but no closet. Nancy could see the gleaming tiles of the bathroom through an open door at the rear of the room. Some papers, pads, and pens were neatly arranged on the desk, and a suitcase lay on the rack next to the closet.

"I'll say one thing for Olmstead. He sure is neat," George commented. She drew in her breath sharply and hurried over to the desk. "Look familiar?" she asked, plucking a bright blue notepad from the pile of items.

"Definitely!" Nancy replied. "Let's see what else we find."

She scanned every square inch and was about to give up searching when she saw the corner of a plastic bag sticking out from beneath one of the beds. Hurrying to the bed, she pulled the bag out and peeked inside. "Computer components," she murmured, frowning. "They're loose—I don't see any indication of what they're for."

"But I bet anything Olmstead has been giving these to Crash to replace AeroTech's components," George said. "Didn't Steven Eriksen tell Admiral Lewis that the malfunctioning component in that simulator that blew up *wasn't* from AeroTech?"

Before Nancy could answer, Richard turned away from the window, where he'd been keeping watch. "Did you say that Bob Olmstead drives a green sedan?" he asked.

"Yes," Nancy told him. "Do you see it?"

Richard backed quickly away from the window. "He's on his way up," he said urgently.

"We've got to get out of here!" George exclaimed. She started for the door, but Richard grabbed her arm.

"There's no time. He'll see us," he told her.

Nancy's eyes flew around the motel room as she shoved the bag of computer components back under the bed. "In the bathroom. Quick!" she said.

The three of them raced for the bathroom doorway, bumping into one another in their haste. By the time they all squeezed inside, Nancy's heart was pounding and she was breathless. George closed the door behind them, and seconds later Nancy heard the scrape of a key in the motel room door. The door opened, and then clanked shut. Olmstead was inside.

Nancy was breathing so hard that she was sure Bob Olmstead would hear her. She just hoped he didn't decide to come into the bathroom! George and Richard were sitting next to each other on the rim of the bathtub. Nancy held her finger to her lips and tried to listen to what Bob Olmstead was doing. She heard the click of his briefcase opening, and then the sound of papers being shuffled. There was a short silence before she heard him say, "Olmstead here. Put me through to Walter Howard, would you?"

Nancy exchanged a wide-eyed glance with George and Richard. Walter Howard? One of the people who ran Howard Technologies?

After a short pause, Bob Olmstead spoke again: "Walt? It's Bob. You wanted me to check in? . . . Yeah, I've run into a little snag, but it'll be taken care of soon. . . . Don't worry about it. I solved the Parker problem, didn't I?"

Nancy had a feeling that what he was really saying was that he had killed Jill. The casual way he talked about it made Nancy's skin crawl.

"I said, don't worry about it," Olmstead repeated, more loudly this time. "Look, it's just a couple of girl trainees. . . . Yeah. . . . My man on the inside is going to take care of them."

Nancy guessed his "man on the inside" was Crash, and that the girl trainees were she and Mary. But she wasn't at all prepared for what she heard next.

"The Chambers girl is already taken care of,"

Olmstead said in a voice that sent shivers down Nancy's spine. "Yeah, same routine as the Parker girl. Her plane might take off in one piece, but something tells me that when it comes back to earth it's going to be in a zillion tiny bits. . . ."

Chapter

Fifteen

NANCY GAPED at George and Richard. Bob Olmstead must have gotten Crash to sabotage Mary's plane!

George caught Nancy's eye and mouthed the question: "Do you think it's too late?"

Nancy knew what she meant: Had Mary taken her plane up yet? Checking her watch, Nancy saw that it was a quarter to two. Mary's session had started at one, but Nancy knew that she and her On Wing would spend about an hour going over material before they took off. There might be just enough time to get to the base and warn Mary—if they could only get out of there!

"Yeah, Walt. Okay," Olmstead's voice cut into her thoughts. "I'll call to let you know when the problems have been taken care of. . . . Sure. . . . 'Bye."

135

A second later Nancy heard the receiver being set back in its cradle. Then she finally heard the motel room door open and shut again. "He's gone!" she whispered.

George jumped for the door, but Nancy held a finger to her lips. Slowly she turned the knob and opened the bathroom door just enough so that she could see into the room. "All clear."

Nancy didn't realize she'd been holding her breath until she let it out. She, George, and Richard all stumbled out of the bathroom. Nancy sprinted for the phone and punched in the number for the base, then gave the extension for the hangar to the operator.

"It's busy!" she groaned, slamming down the receiver.

Richard said, "I'll stay here and try to call security and the hangar, while you two try to get to Mary."

"Leave a message for Admiral Lewis, too," Nancy called over her shoulder as she and George raced for the door. "Then meet us at the south airfield!"

The two girls clattered down the stairs to the parking lot, and moments later Nancy pulled into the street with screeching tires. "Come on," she urged under her breath. She swerved to pass the slow-moving car in front of her, then sped toward the highway. It took all her concentration to keep from driving like a complete maniac. In her mind she kept picturing Mary and her On Wing unaware that anything could be wrong.

"Finally!" George said as the entrance to the base came into sight.

Turning off the highway, Nancy screeched to a stop in front of the security gate. "Call the south field and alert Ensign Mary Chambers not to take off!" Nancy called to the guard. "It's an emergency!"

The guard shot her a dubious look. "And you are . . . ?" he asked.

Nancy groaned and flashed him her pass. "Look, we don't have time for this. *Please,* just do it!" she said. Then she gunned her engine and shot into the base, heading for the south field.

"I hope her plane is still on the ground," George said. She was leaning forward in the passenger seat, her expression worried. "I'll feel awful if—"

She broke off and pointed ahead. "Look! Isn't that plane about to take off?"

The south airfield had just come into view. Nancy could see a T-34C taxiing to the end of the runway. "You're right!" she said. "We've got to stop it!" She didn't even know for sure that Mary was in the plane, but she couldn't take a chance.

Glancing in her rearview mirror, Nancy saw two security vans careening around a corner, heading toward the airstrip, but she wasn't sure they'd make it in time. She pressed down on the car's accelerator, shooting past the hangar and toward the runway. She ignored the waves and shouts of technicians and other trainees near the hangar.

"Driver of the white convertible, halt your vehicle!" an amplified voice came from a speaker on one of the security vans. It was one order Nancy didn't think she could afford to obey.

As they approached the plane on the airstrip, George waved her hands and yelled, "Stop! You're in danger!"

Ahead of them, the noise from the Mentor's engine deepened to supersonic loudness, drowning out George's voice. The plane started to inch forward just as Nancy shot up next to it. She pulled the convertible in a hard right and screeched around in front of the plane. The two security vans were right behind her, lights flashing.

Seconds later the Mentor stopped with its nose just a few yards from the vehicles. The pilot killed the engine, and the cockpit popped open.

"What's going on here!" Nancy recognized Mary's On Wing, Lieutenant Hawkins, as he climbed from the plane, pulling off his helmet. Mary was right behind him. When she saw Nancy and the security vans, a worried frown came over her face.

"Nancy? What happened?" Mary asked. "Is something wrong?"

Nancy jumped out of the convertible and ran over to Mary and Lieutenant Hawkins. Four navy guards from the security vans were right behind them. "If one of you is Mary Chambers, we've received orders to stop your plane from taking off."

Mary's face went completely white, and her On Wing exclaimed, "What!"

"I think Crash sabotaged your plane so that it would blow up while you were in the air," Nancy added.

One of the guards was already ushering the group away from the plane while the others opened the panel to reveal the engine. Nancy turned as a navy jeep drove up to them, with Rhonda Kisch at the wheel. She hopped out and strode over to Nancy. "What's the meaning of this, Ensign Drew?" she snapped angrily.

"Sir!" Nancy snapped a salute. "We have reason to believe that this plane has been sabotaged."

Lieutenant Kisch's expression darkened even more. She strode over to the security force working on Mary's plane and consulted with them for a moment before returning to Nancy's group. "Plastic explosives," the On Wing said. "There's a timer attached. The security force is working to defuse it, but we've all got to stand back."

Nancy was only too happy to obey. While the others started walking toward the hangar, she turned to Mary and asked, "Have you seen Crash around the hangar this afternoon? Do you know if he's been picked up for questioning yet?"

Mary still looked dazed. She simply shrugged and said, "I haven't seen him."

Nancy shaded her eyes and scanned the area near the south field hangar. "I'm going to check the hangar before we try the admiral's office," she said.

She didn't dare get her car yet—it was too near the plastic explosives—so she ran ahead of the others to the hangar. As she moved inside, out of the sun's bright light, it took a few moments for her eyes to adjust to the dimness. She blinked a few times, and when she opened her eyes, she found herself staring right at Crash Beauford.

He was perched in the cockpit of a Mentor right next to the hangar door. For a long moment he met her steady gaze. His blue eyes burned into hers with an intensity that shocked her. She could see the guilt in his eyes—and the desperation. But that didn't stop her heart from beating just a little faster.

"Give it up, Crash," she finally called out. "I know all about what you did. So does Admiral Lewis."

Her voice seemed to snap him into action. In a single swift motion, Crash pulled the cockpit door shut and started the engine. He was still strapping on his helmet when his Mentor jerked forward, straight at Nancy.

He's going to try to get away! she realized.

In a flash she angled out of his way and ran to the nearest Mentor. "No time for a preflight check," she mumbled. "I sure hope this thing is operational!"

As she strapped herself into the safety harness, Nancy checked her gauges, then started the engine. By the time she taxied out of the hangar,

Crash's Mentor was just getting into takeoff position. Nancy headed after him. She neared the runway just as his Mentor whizzed down the airstrip. Before anyone could stop him, his plane arced up over the top of Mary's T-34C, and took off.

"Oh, no!" Nancy said. Seconds later she hit the throttle, and her own plane moved forward. The security crew were waving their arms at her, but Nancy couldn't stop or explain. As she angled into the air, arcing over the surprised group on the airstrip, Crash's plane was just a glint of shiny metal far ahead of her.

Nancy pushed her plane to the standard cruising speed of 170 knots, then to 180. She clicked her radio to the frequency navy pilots used to communicate with one another, then said into her microphone, "Nice flying, Crash, but you're not going to get away."

"Oh, yeah?" his voice came back. Nancy had started to gain, but suddenly he shot farther ahead.

Nancy pushed her T-34C to 190 knots, which allowed her to keep Crash's plane in sight ahead. "I know Bob Olmstead blackmailed you into sabotaging AeroTech's computer simulators," she said into her microphone. "He wrote you instructions and left them in your post office box in town, along with the defective parts you used to replace AeroTech's computer components."

There was a short silence. Then Crash said, "Pretty good guesswork, Ensign."

"It's no guess, Crash," Nancy retorted. "I saw the article on the grade-changing scam *and* one of the notes Olmstead left you. I know Olmstead was using some heavy leverage, but did you have to kill Jill Parker?"

"Jill saw me right after I had put a defective computer component in one of the simulators," Crash's voice came back. "She confronted me about it after the simulator broke down. I talked my way out of it, but I knew she was suspicious. I wouldn't have mentioned it to Olmstead if I thought—"

He broke off, but Nancy knew what he meant. "If you thought he'd order you to kill Jill? Why didn't you go to Admiral Lewis or to your On Wing?"

"You don't get it, do you? My family's been navy for generations," Crash told her. "As far as they're concerned, I'm the best and the brightest the navy will ever see. And I *am* good. I don't deserve to have my whole career ruined just because I made one little mistake."

Nancy couldn't believe he thought his career was important enough to kill other people over. "Killing Jill was a *big* mistake, Crash," she spoke into the microphone. "It's one you're going to be paying for for a long time."

Crash's laugh echoed eerily in Nancy's ears. "You'll have to catch me first," he told her.

Up ahead, sunlight glinted off Crash's wings as the plane twisted in a hard right turn. In a second, Nancy was after him. "Give up, Crash.

They'll go easier on you," she said into her microphone. "Crash?"

Nothing but static came back over the frequency. Crash had turned off his radio. "Fine," she said. "If that's the way you want to play it."

Nancy saw Crash pull his Mentor in a dizzying series of twists. She knew she didn't have the experience to execute such complicated maneuvers at this high speed, but she had to make some turns just to keep his plane in sight. Everything happened so quickly that she hardly knew how she managed to stay in control.

She was just coming out of a hard turn, when Crash's plane seemed to falter ahead of her. "What?" Nancy frowned as Crash's Mentor twisted wildly, wing over wing, for several turns. It looked as if he were out of control!

"Crash! Are you okay?" she spoke urgently into her microphone, but he didn't answer.

Before she could say anything else, Crash's Mentor came out of the spins. Nancy started to sigh with relief, but then she glimpsed the flash of silver shooting toward her at top speed. Crash's plane was about to hit her head-on!

Chapter

Sixteen

Nancy knew she had only a split second before the two planes would collide. All the blood rushed to her feet as she spun the plane in a hard right. The Mentor flipped so sharply that she had no idea where the land, sea, or Crash's plane were.

For the briefest second the entire patch of sky where she was seemed to shake. She knew Crash's plane had to be dangerously close, but she couldn't afford to look around and see where —she had to focus all her energy on flying, or it would be impossible to keep her Mentor under control. Nancy gritted her teeth, half-expecting to be hit. It wasn't until she was flying horizontally again that she saw Crash's plane.

"Oh, no!" she gasped.

His Mentor was spinning out of control again.

144

As she watched, she saw what looked like a small speck pop from the plane's cockpit. Seconds later a parachute billowed out, taking air. Crash had managed to bail out.

Nancy let out a sigh of relief and reached for her radio controls: "Ensign Nancy Drew here. Crash Beauford's Mentor is down, and he's bailed out into the Gulf." Using her navigating equipment, she went on to give the exact coordinates of where Crash was, so that a rescue crew and security force could pick him up.

When she was done, the radio contact at the base told her, "Good job, Ensign. Come on home."

"I still can't believe it," Yolanda Watts said to Nancy that evening at Wings. "Crash killed Jill, and he almost managed to kill you and Mary, too."

"Not to mention that we had a major criminal intrigue going on under our noses and we didn't even know it," Diane Vega added. "I never would have thought that a huge company like Howard Technologies would resort to sabotage and murder in order to get military contracts." She shook her head in amazement.

Nancy, George, Richard Mirsky, Mary, and Steven Eriksen were celebrating the end of the case. Nancy had decided to invite her other two housemates, too, so she could explain what had been going on at the base.

"Bob Olmstead and Walter Howard have both

been arrested for murder, sabotage, and conspiracy to commit murder," Nancy said. "The police don't think anyone else at Howard Technologies is involved, but their investigation is just beginning."

She turned as Admiral Lewis came into Wings and made his way toward their table. A hush fell over the table—it was obvious that the trainees weren't used to seeing Davis Field's top commander in such an informal setting. Several navy personnel started to salute, but the admiral waved his hand and said, "At ease, everyone."

He stopped next to Nancy and said, "I won't be staying, but I thought you'd want to know how Crash's questioning went. He's agreed to testify against Bob Olmstead and Howard Technologies. I made it very clear that that was the only way he wouldn't receive the absolute maximum sentence." He frowned, shaking his head. "It's a shame that such a talented young fighter pilot had his priorities so twisted. Stooping to murder in order to protect his own career—it's an embarrassment to the entire navy."

Nancy felt sorry for the admiral. He seemed to take it personally that Crash wasn't a perfect fighter pilot trainee.

"Thank you for giving me the opportunity to complete my training, Admiral," Mary spoke up from across the table. "It means everything to me." Since her intentions had been good, Admiral Lewis placed Mary on probation but hadn't taken any more serious action.

"I owe some thanks, too," Steven Eriksen spoke up. "I'm very grateful to you for clearing AeroTech's good name." He smiled at Nancy and George as he speared some french fries with his fork. "I knew something fishy was going on, and when I happened to see Bob Olmstead at the beach, I had a feeling that Howard Technologies was behind all of my problems with our computer equipment."

"The police picked Olmstead up at his motel a few hours ago," Nancy told him. "He won't be bothering you anymore."

"You knew Olmstead?" George asked Steven Eriksen.

AeroTech's technical director nodded. "We've run into each other at conferences on computer simulation. By the way," he added, leaning toward Richard Mirsky, "I'd like to give you another demonstration on the computer simulators—*after* I make sure that all the bugs Howard Technologies planted are gone. I want to make sure that AeroTech's image remains untarnished."

"Sure thing," Richard agreed.

"I'm glad we were wrong about AeroTech supplying inferior computer simulators," Admiral Lewis told Steven Eriksen. "But you understand our concern, after hearing about that business in California—"

"That was a fluke," Eriksen insisted. "Aero-Tech made the mistake of getting some computer components from a company that was about to go bankrupt. We didn't know that they had supplied *us* with inferior equipment. The components tested out okay initially, but they didn't hold up under use. Of course we didn't find that out until after the simulators were already operational in the California base. Our technicians were negotiating a new labor contract at the time, so naturally they twisted the story with the press, just to put us in a vulnerable negotiating position."

Mary raised her soda, then grinned around the table. "I'd like to make a toast. Here's to finding out the truth about Jill's death *and* putting the bad guys behind bars."

Nancy turned to clink glasses with George, but she saw that George was busy talking to Richard in low tones. Both of them appeared serious— Nancy guessed that they were realizing that their time together would be over soon. When Richard turned to answer a question Steven Eriksen asked him, George sat back in her chair with a melancholy look on her face.

"Are you okay?" Nancy asked, leaning close to George.

"I guess so." George gave Nancy a weak smile. "Richard's talking about coming to River Heights for a visit after he's done with his article."

Nancy raised an eyebrow at George. "So you've decided that you can live with a long-distance relationship, after all?"

George sighed and took a long sip of her soda.

"I'm not sure. But it didn't seem to make sense to say goodbye for good, either. For now, we're going to leave things open. You know, see each other when we can but not make any big commitment or anything."

"Sounds like a good plan," Nancy said.

She turned as Rhonda Kisch and Lieutenant Hawkins came into Wings and walked over to Nancy's table. After saluting Admiral Lewis, Rhonda turned to Nancy and said, "That was some fine flying you did this afternoon, Nancy."

Nancy noticed that her On Wing didn't call her Ensign anymore. She didn't exactly smile at Nancy, but her face was a little softer than usual.

"Thank you. I never could have done it if you hadn't whipped me into shape," Nancy said truthfully.

"I admit I didn't think much of you when you showed up here," Rhonda said as she and Mary's On Wing pulled chairs up to the table. Then she shined a brilliant smile on Nancy and added, "But now I'm beginning to think you're navy material, after all."

Nancy's next case:

Jealousy. Passion. Ambition. The action on the top-rated soap *Love and Loss* is heating up, and it's all off-camera. In New York City at the invitation of the assistant producer, Nancy is asked to look into a series of damaging leaks revealing the show's future story lines. But her investigation is suddenly interrupted by a shocking development. The program's head writer has been found in his apartment—murdered! Nancy quickly learns that there's no love lost among the cast and crew of *Love and Loss*. Secret schemes and simmering resentments have turned the set into a tangled web of deception and danger. And the killer is preparing one final fatal scene—for Nancy Drew . . . in *Anything for Love,* Case #107 in The Nancy Drew Files™.

For orders other than by individual consumers, Archway Books grants a discount on the purchase of **10 or more** copies of single titles for special markets or premium use. For further details, please write to the Vice-President of Special Markets, Pocket Books, 1230 Avenue of the Americas, New York, NY 10020.

For information on how individual consumers can place orders, please write to Mail Order Department, Paramount Publishing, 200 Old Tappan Road, Old Tappan, NJ 07675.

NANCY DREW® AND
THE HARDY BOYS®
TEAM UP FOR MORE MYSTERY...
MORE THRILLS...AND MORE
EXCITEMENT THAN EVER BEFORE!

A NANCY DREW AND HARDY BOYS
SUPERMYSTERY™

☐ DOUBLE CROSSING	74616-2/$3.99
☐ A CRIME FOR CHRISTMAS	74617-0/$3.99
☐ SHOCK WAVES	74393-7/$3.99
☐ DANGEROUS GAMES	74108-X/$3.99
☐ THE LAST RESORT	67461-7/$3.99
☐ THE PARIS CONNECTION	74675-8/$3.99
☐ BURIED IN TIME	67463-3/$3.99
☐ MYSTERY TRAIN	67464-1/$3.99
☐ BEST OF ENEMIES	67465-X/$3.99
☐ HIGH SURVIVAL	67466-8/$3.99
☐ NEW YEAR'S EVIL	67467-6/$3.99
☐ TOUR OF DANGER	67468-4/$3.99
☐ SPIES AND LIES	73125-4/$3.99
☐ TROPIC OF FEAR	73126-2/$3.99
☐ COURTING DISASTER	78168-5/$3.99
☐ HITS AND MISSES	78169-3/$3.99
☐ EVIL IN AMSTERDAM	78173-1/$3.99
☐ DESPERATE MEASURES	78174-X/$3.99
☐ PASSPORT TO DANGER	78177-4/$3.99
☐ HOLLYWOOD HORROR	78181-2/$3.99
☐ COPPER CANYON CONSPIRACY	88514-6/$3.99
☐ DANGER DOWN UNDER	88460-3/$3.99

Simon & Schuster Mail Order
200 Old Tappan Rd., Old Tappan, N.J. 07675
Please send me the books I have checked above. I am enclosing $_____ (please add $0.75 to cover the postage and handling for each order. Please add appropriate sales tax). Send check or money order–no cash or C.O.D.'s please. Allow up to six weeks for delivery. For purchase over $10.00 you may use VISA: card number, expiration date and customer signature must be included.

Name _____

Address _____

City _____ State/Zip _____

VISA Card # _____ Exp.Date _____

Signature _____ 664-10

THE HARDY BOYS CASEFILES™

☐ #1: DEAD ON TARGET	73992-1/$3.99
☐ #2: EVIL, INC.	73668-X/$3.75
☐ #3: CULT OF CRIME	68726-3/$3.75
☐ #4: THE LAZARUS PLOT	73995-6/$3.75
☐ #5: EDGE OF DESTRUCTION	73669-8/$3.99
☐ #6: THE CROWNING OF TERROR	73670-1/$3.50
☐ #7: DEATHGAME	73672-8/$3.99
☐ #8: SEE NO EVIL	73673-6/$3.50
☐ #9: THE GENIUS THIEVES	73674-4/$3.50
☐ #12: PERFECT GETAWAY	73675-2/$3.50
☐ #13: THE BORGIA DAGGER	73676-0/$3.50
☐ #14: TOO MANY TRAITORS	73677-9/$3.50
☐ #29: THICK AS THIEVES	74663-4/$3.50
☐ #30: THE DEADLIEST DARE	74613-8/$3.50
☐ #32: BLOOD MONEY	74665-0/$3.50
☐ #33: COLLISION COURSE	74666-9/$3.50
☐ #35: THE DEAD SEASON	74105-5/$3.50
☐ #37: DANGER ZONE	73751-1/$3.75
☐ #41: HIGHWAY ROBBERY	70038-3/$3.75
☐ #42: THE LAST LAUGH	74614-6/$3.50
☐ #44: CASTLE FEAR	74615-4/$3.75
☐ #45: IN SELF-DEFENSE	70042-1/$3.75
☐ #47: FLIGHT INTO DANGER	70044-8/$3.99
☐ #48: ROCK 'N' REVENGE	70045-6/$3.50
☐ #49: DIRTY DEEDS	70046-4/$3.99
☐ #50: POWER PLAY	70047-2/$3.99
☐ #52: UNCIVIL WAR	70049-9/$3.50
☐ #53: WEB OF HORROR	73089-4/$3.99
☐ #54: DEEP TROUBLE	73090-8/$3.99
☐ #55: BEYOND THE LAW	73091-6/$3.50
☐ #56: HEIGHT OF DANGER	73092-4/$3.99
☐ #57: TERROR ON TRACK	73093-2/$3.99
☐ #60: DEADFALL	73096-7/$3.99
☐ #61: GRAVE DANGER	73097-5/$3.99
☐ #62: FINAL GAMBIT	73098-3/$3.75
☐ #63: COLD SWEAT	73099-1/$3.75
☐ #64: ENDANGERED SPECIES	73100-9/$3.99
☐ #65: NO MERCY	73101-7/$3.99
☐ #66: THE PHOENIX EQUATION	73102-5/$3.99
☐ #67: LETHAL CARGO	73103-3/$3.75
☐ #68: ROUGH RIDING	73104-1/$3.75
☐ #69: MAYHEM IN MOTION	73105-X/$3.75
☐ #70: RIGGED FOR REVENGE	73106-8/$3.75
☐ #71: REAL HORROR	73107-6/$3.99
☐ #72: SCREAMERS	73108-4/$3.75
☐ #73: BAD RAP	73109-2/$3.99
☐ #74: ROAD PIRATES	73110-6/$3.99
☐ #75: NO WAY OUT	73111-4/$3.99
☐ #76: TAGGED FOR TERROR	73112-2/$3.99
☐ #77: SURVIVAL RUN	79461-2/$3.99
☐ #78: THE PACIFIC CONSPIRACY	79462-0/$3.99
☐ #79: DANGER UNLIMITED	79463-9/$3.99
☐ #80: DEAD OF NIGHT	79464-7/$3.99
☐ #81: SHEER TERROR	79465-5/$3.99
☐ #82: POISONED PARADISE	79466-3/$3.99
☐ #83: TOXIC REVENGE	79467-1/$3.99
☐ #84: FALSE ALARM	79468-X/$3.99
☐ #85: WINNER TAKE ALL	79469-8/$3.99
☐ #86: VIRTUAL VILLAINY	79470-1/$3.99
☐ #87: DEAD MAN IN DEADWOOD	79471-X/$3.99
☐ #88: INFERNO OF FEAR	79472-8/$3.99
☐ #89: DARKNESS FALLS	79473-6/$3.99
☐ #90: DEADLY ENGAGEMENT	79474-4/$3.99
☐ #91: HOT WHEELS	79475-2/$3.99
☐ #92: SABOTAGE AT SEA	79476-0/$3.99
☐ #93: MISSION: MAYHEM	88204-X/$3.99
☐ #94: A TASTE FOR TERROR	88205-8/$3.99
☐ #95: ILLEGAL PROCEDURE	88206-6/$3.99
☐ #96: AGAINST ALL ODDS	88207-4/$3.99
☐ #97: PURE EVIL	88208-2/$3.99
☐ #98: MURDER BY MAGIC	88209-0/$3.99

Simon & Schuster Mail Order
200 Old Tappan Rd., Old Tappan, N.J. 07675

Please send me the books I have checked above. I am enclosing $_____ (please add $0.75 to cover the postage and handling for each order. Please add appropriate sales tax). Send check or money order–no cash or C.O.D.'s please. Allow up to six weeks for delivery. For purchase over $10.00 you may use VISA: card number, expiration date and customer signature must be included.

Name _____

Address _____

City _____ State/Zip _____

VISA Card # _____ Exp.Date _____

Signature _____

762-22

HAVE YOU SEEN THE NANCY DREW FILES™ LATELY?

☐ #1: SECRETS CAN KILL	74674-X/$3.99	☐ #69: CROSSCURRENTS	73072-X/$3.75
☐ #2: DEADLY INTENT	74611-1/$3.75	☐ #70: CUTTING EDGE	73074-6/$3.99
☐ #3: MURDER ON ICE	68729-8/$3.75	☐ #71: HOT TRACKS	73075-4/$3.75
☐ #4: SMILE AND SAY MURDER	73659-0/$3.75	☐ #72: SWISS SECRETS	73076-2/$3.99
☐ #5: HIT AND RUN HOLIDAY	73660-4/$3.99	☐ #73: RENDEZVOUS IN ROME	73077-0/$3.75
☐ #6: WHITE WATER TERROR	73661-2/$3.50	☐ #74: GREEK ODYSSEY	73078-9/$3.75
☐ #8: TWO POINTS FOR MURDER	73663-9/$3.50	☐ #75: A TALENT FOR MURDER	73079-7/$3.99
☐ #9: FALSE MOVES	70493-1/$3.75	☐ #76: THE PERFECT PLOT	73080-0/$3.99
☐ #10: BURIED SECRETS	73664-7/$3.50	☐ #77: DANGER ON PARADE	73081-9/$3.75
☐ #11: HEART OF DANGER	73665-5/$3.50	☐ #79: NO LAUGHING MATTER	73083-5/$3.99
☐ #16: NEVER SAY DIE	73666-3/$3.50	☐ #80: POWER OF SUGGESTION	73084-3/$3.75
☐ #17: STAYED TUNED FOR DANGER	73667-1/$3.50	☐ #81: MAKING WAVES	73085-1/$3.99
		☐ #82: DANGEROUS RELATIONS	73086-X/$3.99
☐ #19: SISTERS IN CRIME	67957-0/$3.75	☐ #83: DIAMOND DECEIT	73087-8/$3.99
☐ #31: TROUBLE IN TAHITI	73912-3/$3.50	☐ #84: CHOOSING SIDES	73088-6/$3.99
☐ #35: BAD MEDICINE	64702-4/$2.95	☐ #85: SEA OF SUSPICION	79477-9/$3.99
☐ #36: OVER THE EDGE	74656-1/$3.50	☐ #86: LET'S TALK TERROR	79478-7/$3.99
☐ #37: LAST DANCE	74657-X/$3.50	☐ #87: MOVING TARGET	79479-5/$3.99
☐ #43: FALSE IMPRESSIONS	74392-9/$3.50	☐ #88: FALSE PRETENSES	79480-9/$3.99
☐ #45: OUT OF BOUNDS	73911-5/$3.50	☐ #89: DESIGNS IN CRIME	79481-7/$3.99
☐ #46: WIN, PLACE OR DIE	67498-6/$3.50	☐ #90: STAGE FRIGHT	79482-5/$3.99
☐ #50: DEEP SECRETS	74525-5/$3.50	☐ #91: IF LOOKS COULD KILL	79483-3/$3.99
☐ #51: A MODEL CRIME	70028-6/$3.75	☐ #92: MY DEADLY VALENTINE	79484-1/$3.99
☐ #53: TRAIL OF LIES	70030-8/$3.75	☐ #93: HOTLINE TO DANGER	79485-X/$3.99
☐ #54: COLD AS ICE	70031-6/$3.50	☐ #94: ILLUSIONS OF EVIL	79486-8/$3.99
☐ #55: DON'T LOOK TWICE	70032-4/$3.75	☐ #95: AN INSTINCT FOR TROUBLE	79487-6/$3.99
☐ #56: MAKE NO MISTAKE	70033-2/$3.50	☐ #96: THE RUNAWAY BRIDE	79488-4/$3.99
☐ #57: INTO THIN ICE	70034-0/$3.50	☐ #97: SQUEEZE PLAY	79489-2/$3.99
☐ #58: HOT PURSUIT	70035-9/$3.99	☐ #98: ISLAND OF SECRETS	79490-6/$3.99
☐ #59: HIGH RISK	70036-7/$3.50	☐ #99: THE CHEATING HEART	79491-4/$3.99
☐ #60: POISON PEN	70037-5/$3.50	☐ #100: DANCE TILL YOU DIE	79492-2/$3.99
☐ #61: SWEET REVENGE	73065-7/$3.50	☐ #101: THE PICTURE OF GUILT	88192-2/$3.99
☐ #62: EASY MARKS	73066-5/$3.50	☐ #102: COUNTERFEIT CHRISTMAS	88193-0/$3.99
☐ #63: MIXED SIGNALS	73067-3/$3.50	☐ #103: HEART OF ICE	88194-9/$3.99
☐ #64: THE WRONG TRACK	73068-1/$3.99	☐ #104: KISS AND TELL	88195-7/$3.99
☐ #65: FINAL NOTES	73069-X/$3.75	☐ #105: STOLEN AFFECTIONS	88196-5/$3.99
☐ #66: TALL, DARK, AND DEADLY	73070-3/$3.99	☐ #106: FLYING TOO HIGH	88197-3/$3.99

Available from Archway Paperbacks
Published by Pocket Books

Simon & Schuster Mail Order
200 Old Tappan Rd., Old Tappan, N.J. 07675
Please send me the books I have checked above. I am enclosing $_____ (please add $0.75 to cover the postage and handling for each order. Please add appropriate sales tax). Send check or money order-no cash or C.O.D.'s please. Allow up to six weeks for delivery. For purchase over $10.00 you may use VISA: card number, expiration date and customer signature must be included.

Name _____

Address _____

City _____ State/Zip _____

VISA Card # _____ Exp.Date _____

Signature _____

766-21

COLOMA PUBLIC LIBRARY